Other books by Christine and Christopher Russell

The Quest of the Warrior Sheep
The Warrior Sheep Go West
The Warrior Sheep Down Under

The Warrior SHEEP Go Jurassic

CHRISTINE & CHRISTOPHER RUSSELL

JF
M/M 4783
7.99
8/18

EGMONT

This book is dedicated to our good friends Christine and John.

EGMONT

The Warrior Sheep Go Jurassic
First published in Great Britain 2013
by Jelly Pie – an imprint of Egmont UK Limited
The Yellow Building, 1 Nicholas Road, London W11 4AN

Text copyright © Christine and Christopher Russell 2013

The moral rights of the authors and cover illustrator have been asserted

ISBN 978 1 4052 6718 2

1 3 5 7 9 10 8 6 4 2

A CIP catalogue record for this title is available from the British Library

Typeset by Avon DataSet Ltd, Bidford on Avon, Warwickshire
Printed and bound in Great Britain by the CPI Group

54947/1

Stay safe online. Any website addresses listed in this book are correct at the time of
going to print. However, Egmont is not responsible for content hosted by third parties.
Please be aware that online content can be subject to change and websites can contain
content that is unsuitable for children. We advise that all children are supervised when
using the internet.

EGMONT LUCKY COIN

Our story began over a century ago, when seventeen-year-old
Egmont Harald Petersen found a coin in the street.

He was on his way to buy a flyswatter, a small hand-operated
printing machine that he then set up in his tiny apartment.

The coin brought him such good luck that today Egmont has
offices in over 30 countries around the world. And that lucky
coin is still kept at the company's head offices in Denmark.

Contents

1
The Dragon

It was a dragon. Definitely a dragon.

Sal had never seen one before but she knew exactly what it was. The huge jaws, the rows of sharp teeth, the scaly skin, the claws. She knew because the Songs of the Fleece spoke of a terrifying beast just like it. And the Songs of the Fleece were never wrong. Sal backed away from the side of the trailer she was standing in.

Wills, the youngest of the five Rare Breed sheep from Eppingham Farm, noticed, and trotted over to her side.

'What's the matter, Sal?' he asked. 'Are you still feeling seasick?'

'No, dear,' replied Sal, her eyes fixed on the dragon. 'Not now we're out in the fresh air again . . .'

Wills followed her gaze, but he couldn't see what

was bothering her, so he stuck his head through the bars of the trailer for a better look. He found himself staring at a banner fixed to railings at the side of the road. A very long and colourful banner. He turned his head first left, then right, trying to work out what the picture was supposed to show. Some sort of monster, for sure. With a huge egg tucked between its clawed feet. There were words too, but before Wills could begin working out what they said the trailer jolted forward. It jolted again and the banner was left behind as the battered old van, towing the trailer full of sheep, clattered up the slip road away from the ferry. On to the Isle of Wight.

Inside the van, Ida White was trying not to get too excited. She kept reminding herself that she mustn't wave her hands around or bounce up and down while she was driving. Her grandson, Tod, couldn't bounce about either, but only because he was sitting squashed tightly between a dozen bags full of stuff for making carnival costumes: reels of wire, sticky tape, colourful fabrics and feathers. He was excited too. He'd often helped his gran run costume-making workshops. She was brilliant at it: astronauts, giant birds, knights on horseback. Nothing was too difficult for Gran. But this was the first time they'd been invited to lead a workshop on the Isle of Wight.

The invitation had come right out of the blue towards the end of the summer holidays. An email from somebody called Rex Headland had pinged into Ida's inbox. She'd found it when she went to the barn to feed the hens. She often left her laptop in the barn playing music for the hens. They seemed to like it. The email had explained that most towns on the Isle of Wight held a carnival every year and that the town of Ventnor wanted theirs to be especially good this year. Better than all the others. They couldn't afford to pay Ida a fee for teaching them to make the most fabulous float with fabulous costumes to match, but they *could* offer her a nice little flat in the town for the week and pay her ferry fare.

'Well, what do you think?' Ida had asked Tod.

Tod had checked the map. 'Ventnor's right on the south coast of the island,' he said. 'It's got a beach and cliffs and fishing boats and ice-cream shops . . . . It could be brilliant.' He paused. 'But, Gran, we can't accept. We couldn't leave the sheep for a whole week.'

'No . . . no, we couldn't.' Ida shooed a few hens out of the way and sat down on a hay bale. She put the laptop on her lap and began to type.

> Dear Mr Headland,
>
> My grandson Tod and I would love to accept your
> offer but unfortunately we have a problem: our
> little flock of five Rare Breed sheep. Could you,
> by any chance, offer them accommodation too?
> Yours hopefully,
> Ida White

The answer came back within minutes.

> Dear Ida,
>
> Fred Jolliff says they can stay with his flock
> at Home Farm. That's about two miles from
> Ventnor. Fred says the grass is good.
> Yours also hopefully,
> Rex Headland
> (Chairman of the Carnival Committee)

Gran looked at Tod. Tod grinned back.

'Book the ferry, Gran,' he cried as they high-fived. 'Carnival here we come!'

And so, a few days later, Tod was making sandwiches for the journey: cheese, mustard and jam on brown bread. Their favourite. He also put in a bag of fresh raspberries he'd picked and a slab of Gran's mystery cake. All her cakes were a mystery. She made up the recipes as she went long. This one looked to have quite a lot of dates in it. And possibly peas.

Outside, Ida had filled the old trailer with straw and thrown in a lot of cabbages.

She gave a piercing whistle through her fingers. 'Come on, sheep,' she called. 'Time to go.'

Oxo, the big white and black Oxford ram, didn't need any persuading to get into the trailer. Cabbages, a cauliflower too . . . what more could he ask for? Food was always the first thing on Oxo's mind. Usually the second and third as well. He was followed closely by Links, the Lincoln Longwool. Links had a long, curly fleece that danced and jiggled around as he moved.

'Hey, you eatin' it all, innit,' he said as he jumped in beside Oxo. 'Move over, man.'

Sal clambered in slowly. She was a fat Southdown ewe, not very athletic, with a thick, creamy coloured fleece.

'Now, now, don't squabble, boys,' she said. Then she settled on the comfy straw bedding, wondering where they were going and if she'd have time to teach Wills a few verses from the Songs of the Fleece.

Wills, the skinny, black and white Welsh Balwen lamb, sprang in next. Wills was an orphan and had been brought up in Ida's kitchen. He knew a lot about human ways and could even read a little, as he'd often sat with Tod while the boy was doing his homework. Tod was ten years old and had quite a lot of homework.

Wills bounced excitedly up and down. He loved an adventure. 'Get a move on, Jaycey,' he called. 'Or we'll go without you.'

Jaycey, a pretty little Jacob sheep, was sulking at the other end of the paddock. She was enjoying posing in the sunshine and didn't see why she should have to go anywhere. But she didn't want to be left behind either, so she trotted over to the trailer and leapt in, landing lightly on her dainty hooves.

Ida shut the trailer's tailgate and bolted it securely. You could never be too careful with this little bunch.

A few minutes later they were on the road, heading south towards the city of Portsmouth and its harbour.

When they got there, Tod and Ida were surprised at how many cars and lorries and coaches were already lined up on the quayside.

'Surely we won't all get on to one boat?' said Tod.

But the ferry that arrived from the Isle of Wight was huge. Hundreds of cars drove slowly off and away up the slip road. When it was time to load the vehicles going to the Island, Ida drove carefully up the steep ramp and on to the car deck.

'Phew,' she said when they finally stopped behind a coach full of excited children.

'Nice driving, Gran,' said Tod.

They were both a bit disappointed that the sheep had to stay in their trailer while the ferry was at sea.

'If dogs are allowed on the passenger decks, why not sheep?' Ida had asked one of the deckhands.

'Might frighten the dogs,' he replied.

He wasn't serious but the sheep had to stay where they were.

Still, it wasn't a long crossing, less than an hour. Tod and Ida stood by the rail, watching the mainland slip away and then the Island get closer. They enjoyed the sun and the salt spray on their faces as they chomped their sandwiches.

In their trailer on the car deck, the sheep settled down on the straw and dozed in the semi-darkness. All except Sal who felt slightly seasick.

The sheep had been to sea before. They'd crossed oceans. But none of Sal's stomachs had ever got used to it.

Soon though, there was a gentle bump as the ferry docked and then Ida was driving carefully down the ramp on to the Isle of Wight. She joined a slow-moving queue of vehicles that had left the ferry ahead of them and stop-started up the narrow slip road. The railings at the edge of the road were festooned with banners advertising Island attractions: Carisbrooke Castle, Alum Bay, the Sandy Bay Dinosaur Museum. Tod gazed at them all eagerly. Especially the huge picture of a dinosaur.

At the end of the slip road Ida turned on to the main road and followed the sign for Ventnor.

'Are they OK?' she asked for the tenth time as she put her foot on the accelerator.

Tod pushed aside a bunch of very long, green feathers that was tickling his nose and twisted round again so that he could just see through the back of the van into the trailer.

'They look fine, Gran,' he said. 'We've definitely done the right thing bringing them.'

Ida wound down the window so that the wind blew through their hair and she had to shout to be heard. 'Absolutely!'

They didn't need to tell each other exactly *why*: the fact that their little flock of Rare Breeds had a habit of disappearing whenever their backs were turned. In the past, the sheep had made their way North to Scotland, West to the United States and all the way Down Under to Australia. Tod and Ida had never found out how.

The trailer was bumping from side to side as Ida drove faster. Wills was braced on his feet, staring at Sal. The others were too. Sal was sitting very still with her head up and her eyes tight shut.

'What's the matter?' asked Oxo. 'Here, have a cabbage.' He nudged the last one, big and juicy, over to her. 'That'll cheer you up.'

Links shook his head and his curls flopped gently from side to side.

'Na . . .' he said sagely. 'It ain't hunger. It's the Songs of the Fleece, innit.'

Sal's eyes slowly opened. 'It is indeed the Songs of the Fleece,' she whispered. 'The ancient songs of our sheeply tribe. The songs that remind us of our noble history. *And* tell us of what is still to come.' She heaved herself to her feet and announced in a loud voice, 'Verses three hundred and nine and three hundred and ten.'

'Oh, purleeeze,' groaned Jaycey. 'Purleeeze' was a new word she was trying out for size, hoping it made her sound more grown up and sophisticated and bored.

Sal pretended she hadn't heard. She cleared her throat and began to recite:

'Only the few will understand
A picture spied twixt sea and land.

A dragon with . . .'

'A *dragon*?' Wills was so surprised his voice squeaked. 'I thought it was a dinosaur.'

'A what?' Sal hated being interrupted when she was reciting. She glared at Wills.

'A dinosaur,' he said apologetically.

'And what exactly is *that*?'

'Well, they're not anything now. They're extinct. That's why there's a museum all about them. But they lived millions of years ago and . . .'

Sal wasn't looking impressed.

Wills stumbled on. 'They had lots of teeth and scaly skin and claws and . . .'

'And did they lay eggs?' Sal demanded.

Wills gulped. He thought so but he couldn't remember. They didn't look as if they did. In fact, he was beginning to realise that he didn't know much at all about dinosaurs. Or dragons for that matter.

'Erm . . .'

'But you *do* agree that the *dragon*,' Sal emphasised the word, 'in the picture we saw back there, had an egg between its feet?'

Wills couldn't argue with that. 'Yes.'

'An egg?' Oxo was getting confused. 'I thought only hens laid eggs.'

'Dragons lay eggs too,' Sal told him firmly. 'And if you'll only *listen* to me,' she glared at them one by one, 'you will see how important that is.' She cleared her throat, loudly, and began again.

'Only the few will understand
A picture spied twixt sea and land.
A dragon with scaly skin and claws,
Crushing teeth in vicious jaws.
Oh woe is you, for you have seen
A dragon: fierce and cruel and mean.'

'Ohmygrass . . .' whimpered Jaycey. 'We haven't got to go slaying monsters again, have we?'

'Nah . . .' whispered Links. 'We been there, done that, innit.'

Sal paused.

'Is that it?' asked Oxo. 'Only if you don't want that cabbage . . .'

'*Listen!*' shouted Sal. So they did.

'But though this dragon has now died,
As dragons have the whole world wide,
She left an egg within which lies
Dragons enough to fill the skies!
To fill the world with foulest breath
With fire and famine and awful death . . .'

The others were staring at Sal in silence. Fearful silence. Was it to be monster-slaying after all? Sal intoned,

'Step forward, Warriors, if you dare
The planet's fate is in your care.
Your boldest deeds you now must match.
This dragon's egg must never hatch!'

She sat down heavily and closed her eyes.

There was a short silence. Then Oxo sniffed.

'Well I don't reckon much of that,' he said. 'I thought you were going to tell us about something really big and dangerous. We're supposed to be the Warrior Sheep! What's hard about crushing an egg?'

Wills had got over feeling upset that Sal had been

cross with him. He was very excited now.

'We've got to *find* it first,' he said, his eyes shining. 'That could be the hardest bit. It could be *anywhere*!'

The sheep spent the rest of the journey trying to imagine where a dragon might have left her egg. But they hadn't got much beyond barns or hen houses when the van turned off the road and came to a clattery halt. They crowded to the side of the trailer and peered through the bars. They were in a huge field which sloped gently uphill towards the skyline. It was dotted with large, leafy trees, beneath which sat sheep, chewing the cud. Hundreds more sheep were grazing or tugging at bales of hay or just standing around.

Tod suddenly appeared and opened the tailgate of the trailer.

'Here we are, guys,' he called. 'Penny Pasture. Your holiday home for the week.' One by one, the sheep jumped from the trailer on to the soft grass.

'Nice . . .' mumbled Oxo through a mouthful. 'Very nice.'

But Wills was on his toes, alert and trembling slightly.

'Not yet, Oxo,' he said quietly. 'Come with me. But look natural.'

The others didn't know what he meant by 'look natural' but they followed anyway.

As they wandered away, a small, sun-tanned man in patched-up clothes and Wellington boots was helping Ida climb down from the van.

'I told ol' Rex they can stay for a week, but they can stay as long as you likes,' he said. 'There's plenty o' grass for five visters. Prime grazin' Penny Pasture is.'

'It's very kind of you, Mr Jolliff,' said Ida. 'How many times a day do you come into the pasture to check your sheep?'

'A day?' Fred Jolliff's eyes opened wide. 'There be no time to check 'em every day.'

'Oh.' Ida looked worried.

'It be summer. I drives *past* every day and gives 'em a quick look over, o'course. From the road. And I checks the water trough's clean every couple o' days. They don't need no more than that. They be happy as Larry out here.'

Ida suddenly felt a bit foolish. She was talking to a proper farmer with hundreds of sheep. Of course he didn't check on each one of them a dozen times a day as she and Tod did with their little flock.

'Well,' she said, getting straight back into the van. 'We're very grateful to you. Aren't we, Tod?'

Tod nodded and climbed in beside her. 'They'll be fine, Gran,' he whispered. 'Let's go.'

Ida turned the van and drove out of the field, back on to the road. Fred Jolliff followed her out in his truck and bolted the gate.

'Good luck with the float and the costumes an' that,' he called.

A tear escaped and rolled down Ida's wrinkled cheeks as she drove, but she brushed it roughly away.

'I'm being *so* silly,' she said. 'They'll be fine. Safe as sausages. With all those other lovely sheep in that lovely field . . .'

But even as she spoke, Oxo was barging through a gap in the hedge on the far side of the lovely field. It hadn't been a gap before he started on it.

'It's a bit tight,' he grunted, shoving his great head harder into the thicket of broken branches and leaves and rusty barbed wire. Gradually he bored a hole big enough for his shoulders to go through and the rest of his body followed easily. Sal went next. She was quite a bit fatter and Links had to shove her from behind.

16

Links himself squeezed through without effort, and Jaycey and Wills barely touched the sides. Fred Jolliff's sheep merely munched and watched and shook their heads.

'I hope you've got a good reason for making us do this, tin-ribs,' growled Oxo, twitching away dry twigs that had snagged in the fleece around his nose. 'That grass back there was super tasty.'

'I have,' said Wills quickly, before Jaycey could start complaining about her fleece getting messed up. 'I really have. Look!'

They were standing on a footpath and they all looked up at the signpost in front of them. It had two wooden arms. The writing on one arm had worn away. But the words on the other arm had been repainted and were perfectly clear, even from a distance.

'What does it say, dear?' asked Sal. 'What's it pointing to?'

The words burst out of the excited lamb.

'The Dragon's Nest!' cried Wills. 'It's pointing to The Dragon's Nest!'

2
Chas and Arnie

'The Isle of Wight is about twenty-seven miles long and fifteen miles wide,' said Chas Thickett.

He was sitting comfortably in the passenger lounge of an Isle of Wight ferry. Well away from the other passengers. It was just an hour after the sheep had made their crossing and Chas was reading aloud from the screen of his laptop. His younger brother, Arnie, was sitting opposite, trying not to listen. He usually tried not to listen when Chas was in the middle of one of his brainwaves. They always ended in disaster. Sometimes prison.

Arnie yawned and glanced out of the window at the waves lapping gently against the side of the car ferry. The sea beyond was dark and still. Its surface rippled like a half-set jelly. The sun had gone down, and looking back, he could see the lights of Portsmouth

18

twinkling along the coast of the mainland. He wished he were still there. Or at home in London. He didn't like boats or the sea any more than he liked Chas's get-rich-quick schemes.

'At its closest point, the Island is three miles from the mainland, and is served by regular ferry connections,' read Chas. 'It has a population of about one hundred and fifty thousand people. It is a popular destination for holidaymakers.'

'I *wish* . . .' muttered Arnie. 'I haven't been on holiday for years.'

'Stop moaning and listen,' said Chas. 'If my little plan works, you could be on holiday for the rest of your life.'

'Or inside,' said Arnie.

'Shushh!' Chas glanced round to make sure nobody had heard.

He beckoned his brother to lean forward and look at the screen.

'Now this is the interesting bit,' he said. He read quickly and quietly, running his finger along the lines of words on the screen. '"The Island's diverse geology contains a wealth of fossils. And, because the ground is soft and erodes easily, *new* fossils are being exposed all the time."' Chas paused and looked at Arnie. 'How about that?' He was trying hard to get Arnie interested. He couldn't carry out the job he had in mind without his brother, and a willing Arnie would be much better than a grumpy one.

Arnie leaned over the laptop, reaching for a plastic cup of coffee on the table. Crumbs of bread and cheese fell from the sandwich he was holding in his other hand on to the keyboard. 'So?' he said.

Chas brushed the crumbs off, tutting. 'So . . .' he said brightly. '*Why* are so many dinosaurs buried on the Isle of Wight?'

Arnie yawned and took a bite of sandwich. 'I dunno but I expect you're gonna tell me.'

Chas was indeed. He continued as if he were reading an exciting adventure story. Which in a way, he was.

'"Over one hundred and twenty *million* years ago, it was much warmer on the Island than it is now. Plants flourished and provided food for plant-eating dinosaurs. These creatures travelled together in herds as protection from the *meat*-eating dinosaurs that hunted them."' He glanced up. Arnie was leaning back, more interested in his sandwich.

'Like Neovenator Salerii, for example,' announced Chas.

'Come again?' said Arnie.

Chas sighed and continued reading. '"Neovenator Salerii, pronounced *knee-oh-vena-tour sall-air-ee-eye*, was a large-bodied, meat-eating dinosaur. It walked on its long hind legs and had three clawed toes on each foot. It probably had three digits on each hand. It had a long body and a long tail. The mouth was full of blade-like serrated teeth, and above the eyes it had horned extensions of the skull."' He looked up. 'It was a mighty beast, Arnie. Eight metres. And the first one ever found was dug up on the Isle of Wight.'

'Yeah, yeah. Just wake me up when you get to a bit that concerns *me*,' Arnie said, and he settled himself into his comfy padded bench seat and closed his eyes. He had never shared his brother's enthusiasm for fossils and dinosaurs and could think of few things more boring than reading about them online for hours on end.

Chas wasn't going to be put off though. He *was*

genuinely interested in dinosaurs and enjoyed reading about them. But he liked money even more and suddenly, just this morning, he'd come across a way of combining the two. Money and dinosaurs. Big time.

He'd come across the website of the Sandy Bay Dinosaur Museum. And the web page which was in front of him now. He'd read and re-read this page many times in the last few hours. And each time, he'd wondered how the website owners could have made such a stupid mistake. He read on, silently now, to see if the information that should never have been there had finally been taken down.

Here at the Sandy Bay Dinosaur Museum we are constantly finding new specimens and we have many remains which are as yet a mystery. Recent finds include:

Dinosaur teeth
Sections of vertebrae
Claws
A section of hip bone
A small section of thigh bone

Chas peered at the screen. Double checked. But no! It wasn't there any more. Someone *had* spotted the mistake. Someone had removed news of *the* most interesting of all the recent finds. The *dinosaur egg*! The egg, which might have been laid by a Neovenator Salerii, one hundred and twenty million years ago, was no longer listed.

But too late. Chas smiled and patted his breast pocket smugly. It *had* been listed. And he, sharp-eyed Chas Thickett, had seen it. And printed it off. He smiled again.

'Ladies and gentlemen,' a loud voice boomed from the ferry's speaker system, making Chas jump. 'We will shortly be arriving at our Isle of Wight terminal. Will all drivers and passengers please return to their vehicles.'

Arnie opened his eyes. He hadn't been asleep, just ignoring Chas going on about Neoventilatorwhatsits. 'Who's driving? You or me?'

'You are,' said Chas. 'I'm still thinking.' He closed his laptop carefully, then stood up and put on the tweed jacket that had been lying on the seat beside him.

Arnie, who was swigging the last mouthful of his

coffee, snorted with laughter and a few drops of coffee escaped from his nose and hit the table. He wiped them off with his sleeve.

'Nice jacket, bruv,' he said.

Chas scowled at him. 'I'm blending in, Arnie, blending in. Just like Dad always told us.'

'You call that blending in?'

Chas nodded. 'According to my research, going to the Isle of Wight is like stepping back in time. The pace of life is slower, it's peaceful and almost crime-free.'

Arnie snorted again. 'No doubt you're planning to change that.'

He stood up and rolled his shoulders. He was wearing black cycling shorts and a lime green lycra cycling vest.

Chas glared at him. 'Haven't you got anything to change into? You'll stand out like a sore thumb dressed like that.'

'If I don't wear my padded shorts, I'll end up with a sore bum,' said Arnie.

Chas stared. 'You're not telling me you've brought your bike?'

'Course I have.' Arnie grinned. 'They had bikes as well as tweed jackets back in the day, didn't they?'

'Not state-of-the-art racers,' grunted Chas as he stalked towards the staircase. He followed the other passengers down to the car deck.

The evening air was soft and warm and a few stars were twinkling in the darkening sky. Chas squirmed between parked cars, heading for the van that wasn't exactly theirs. Sure enough, Arnie's bike was fixed to the back.

'It was there when we left home,' said Arnie, as he climbed into the driving seat. 'If you weren't always "thinking", you'd have seen it.'

Arnie was right. Chas had been too busy plotting to notice the bike earlier. Or indeed the van itself. Now Chas was worried. The wording displayed in bold lettering on the side of the van read:

MR FIXALL
NO JOB TOO SMALL OR TOO LARGE

'Where did you get this from?' he asked sharply as he climbed into the passenger seat.

Arnie buckled his seat belt. 'Borrowed it from a guy down the road.'

'Does he know?' said Chas suspiciously.

Arnie shrugged. 'He's on holiday. Spain for two weeks. It'll be back outside his house before he gets home. He'll be none the wiser.'

Chas drew a deep breath. 'I thought you were going to hire one.'

'You didn't give me any money,' said Arnie. 'And besides, you're not the only one who remembers what Dad taught us.'

'Meaning?'

'Meaning that if I'd hired a van, the garage would have wanted my name and address and stuff like that. This way, if anything goes wrong, the police won't be able to trace us, or rather *me*, through the vehicle.'

'Not unless someone saw you "borrowing" it,' said Chas. Then he brightened up. 'Anyway, nothing's going to go wrong. Not if you do as I say.'

'Yeah, right.' Arnie didn't sound convinced. 'Anyway, *Dad* said we should always cover our tracks. Lay false trails. And that's what I've done. The trail to this van leads to Mr Fixall down the road, not to me.'

He switched on the engine and followed the car in front down the ramp and on to the Isle of Wight.

Chas was quietly impressed. Despite the sulking, Arnie seemed to be taking things seriously for once. Chas glanced out of the window. They were driving slowly past a banner attached to railings at the side of the road. It showed a picture of a long-necked dinosaur. One with green scaly skin, sharp teeth and claws. And an egg between its feet. Above it were the words:

SANDY BAY DINOSAUR MUSEUM

Come and see our amazing collection of fossils

Learn about the dinosaurs that used to roam this island

For opening times and further information see:

www.sandybaydinosaurs.com

'Yes!' Chas did a little jiggle in his seat. 'We're on our way.' He laughed. 'But we don't do opening times.'

Arnie glanced sideways at his brother. 'What are you on about now?'

'I'll tell you later,' said Chas. 'Follow the signs to Sandy Bay. We're heading for the dinosaur museum.'

'Dinosaur museum?' Arnie raised his eyes but did as he was told. 'You're not suggesting we spend the night in a museum?'

'Not the *whole* night,' replied Chas, grinning broadly. 'Just a little bit of it. For the rest, I've booked us into a nice little pub. According to the guide book, they do a very good bed and breakfast.' He sat back to enjoy the ride. 'Very convenient that, the pub being almost opposite the museum.'

'What's the pub called then?' asked Arnie. 'The T Rex and Lettuce?'

'Ho, ho,' said Chas. 'Very funny. No. It's called The Dragon's Nest.'

3
The Egg

It took the sheep a long time to reach The Dragon's Nest. And when they did, Wills was bitterly disappointed. It wasn't a nest at all.

They had followed the footpath from the signpost outside Penny Pasture through endless fields of wheat and barley and one of cabbages. Oxo had snaffled one small, rather unripe cabbage as they passed but Wills wouldn't let him stop for a proper feed. The sun was going down, it was gradually getting darker and Wills was eager to press on.

'We must be nearly there,' he said, as they struggled along a path overgrown with nettles and brambles. For once he was in the lead and he was enjoying the experience. Almost as much as he was enjoying the excitement of the hunt. But from the silence behind him, Wills could tell that the others weren't enjoying it quite so much.

Finally the little flock emerged from the overgrown path on to a road.

'Which way now, dear?' asked Sal wearily.

'Erm . . .' Wills looked left and right.

'Oh, purl*eeeze*,' said Jaycey, dramatically. 'Don't tell us you don't know.'

'Erm . . .' Wills looked left again. It was completely dark now. All he could see was one building a little further along the road. Warm, welcoming light shone from all its windows and fairy lights twinkled around the door. 'This way,' he said, trying to sound more confident than he felt.

They trotted quickly towards the building.

'Ohmygrass!' Jaycey stopped abruptly and stared.

A painted dragon, with an egg between its clawed feet, covered the whole side wall of the building.

'Ohmygrass . . .' Jaycey said again. 'Is this where it lives then?'

'Got to be, innit?' said Links.

'Easy-peasy, cabbage leavesy,' said Oxo. 'Well done, tin-ribs.'

'Yes, well *done*, dear,' said Sal. 'You have led us straight to our goal.'

Wills dropped his head. 'Erm . . . I don't think so,' he said quietly.

'What's that, dear?' said Sal. 'Speak up.'

'This isn't a dragon's nest,' Wills admitted miserably. 'Not a *real* one. It's just a pub.'

He read aloud the words under the picture of the dragon.

The Dragon's Nest
One of the oldest pubs on the Island
And the best!
Food served all day
Two delightful letting rooms
Large garden
Coaches, dogs and children welcome

Wills sighed. 'It's just a place where humans come to eat and drink.'

'Ohmy*grass* . . .' Jaycey flopped to the ground. 'You're telling us we've walked all this way to a place where *dogs* are welcome?'

Wills nodded, too embarrassed and ashamed to speak.

'Let up, Jaycey,' said Links. 'Any dude can make a mistake. And Wills is only little, innit.' He gave the sad lamb a friendly nudge.

'Yes, there's no need to make a fuss,' said Sal, hiding her own disappointment. She looked around. 'But I really must sit down soon.'

'Maybe the garden?' suggested Wills. 'Away from the road.'

If any of the pub's customers had looked out of the window, they would have seen five tired sheep trotting across the car park. But nobody looked up from their evening meal and the Warriors arrived unseen around the far side of the building. They found a nice soft patch of grass near the hedge, beside a wooden table, and settled down to sleep.

'I'm sorry,' said Wills for the umpteenth time. 'I should have known it wouldn't be that easy.'

He was answered by four loud snores. He closed his own eyes and was soon snoring too.

A few minutes later, Chas and Arnie Thickett drew into

the car park of The Dragon's Nest. Arnie parked their van, leapt to the ground and did a few star jumps to loosen his stiff muscles. Chas climbed down, clutching his laptop. He peered across the road at the dim outline of a building opposite.

'There you go . . .' he said, pleased with himself. 'That must be the dinosaur museum.' He turned and marched towards the pub. 'Right, Arnie. If anyone asks, we're here on holiday. Got that? Holiday.' He lowered his voice. 'And remember. Try to blend in. We don't want to be noticed.'

He marched to the front door. It burst open just as he reached it and a small group of cheerful people tumbled out.

'Oops, sorry,' said the young woman at the front of the group. She stood aside to let Chas pass. She was dressed in exactly the same sort of clothes that young women in London wore.

'Nice jacket,' she said with a giggle. 'Going to a fancy dress party?'

Chas opened and closed his mouth.

'The apple pie's good tonight,' said the girl as she walked away.

'You're blending in well,' said Arnie as he followed Chas into the pub.

Once they'd found the reception desk and checked in, the landlady showed them to their room.

'I noticed your van,' she said. 'You couldn't fix a leaking tap for me could you, Mr Fixall?'

'Yes,' said Arnie.

'No,' said Chas.

The landlady looked from one to the other. 'I'll take that as a "don't know", shall I?'

'Sorry.' Chas smiled apologetically. 'We're here on holiday, you see. Trying to chillax, take it easy, that kind of thing.'

The landlady shrugged. 'No problem. I've reserved you a table for dinner.' She turned at the bedroom door. 'But the apple pie's all gone.'

Even without the apple pie, the meal was good. Chas picked at a plate of fish and chips while Arnie tucked into a huge steak and kidney pie.

'You're eating too much,' said Chas, quietly. 'You've gotta be alert and supple for this job, not fat and dozy.'

'Fat?' said Arnie loudly, through a mouthful of mashed potato.

'Sshh . . .' Chas glanced round at the other diners but they were all busy with their own conversations. None of them had looked up at Arnie's indignant voice. 'Remember what Dad told us,' whispered Chas. 'Never draw attention to yourself before a job.'

'When have I ever been fat?' Arnie was still glaring at Chas. 'I'm a lean, mean fighting machine.' He patted his stomach. 'All muscle, that is.' He took another mouthful of pie and mashed spud. 'Anyway, now we're here, are you finally gonna tell me what this is all about?'

'Finish your dinner first,' said Chas. 'You never could do two things at once.'

He sat and waited patiently while Arnie chomped. His lowered eyes darted this way and that, watching the comings and goings in the dining room. Hadn't his old dad always said to make a note of every detail? To know who was where and what was what?

Their table looked out on to the side garden of the pub. Chas glanced out of the window. The garden was in darkness except for the faint light that reached it from the car park. He turned back to his brother. Then did a double take. He looked out of the window again sharply. Put his nose close to the glass and peered out.

'What's the matter?' asked Arnie, mopping his plate with a doorstep of bread. 'Seen a dinosaur?'

Chas pushed his chair back and stood up. 'Wait here,' he said. 'There's something weird out there. Five white lumps of . . . I dunno what. I'm gonna check it out.' He hurried away.

Arnie shrugged and ordered treacle tart and custard for pudding.

The pub garden was still and quiet when Chas crept round the corner. Quiet that is, except for a series of low, rumbling sounds. He stood listening, his body tense. The noise continued, punctuated by the occasional drawn-out whistle. It was definitely coming from the white lumps lying in the shelter of the hedge. His mind flicked to red alert. Undercover policemen? Maybe they'd been tipped off about his planned raid on the museum.

Don't be so stupid, he silently told himself. Nobody knew about the raid. Not even Arnie. And why were they dressed in white? He crept across the grass towards the lumps. His nose wrinkled as he got closer. They didn't smell like policemen. A few steps closer and he saw why. They weren't policemen. They were sheep. Five assorted sheep, lying close together and snoring peacefully. Chas turned and stumped away.

Countryside, he reminded himself. *You have to be prepared for anything out here.*

Arnie had just finished his pudding and was about to order coffee and cake when Chas returned.

'No time for that,' Chas told him. He paid the bill, fake yawning loudly as he did so.

'It's been a busy day,' he told the landlady. 'We need a good long sleep. We won't be disturbed, will we?'

'I shouldn't think so,' she replied. 'It's as silent as the grave around here once we've closed.'

'I thought we weren't supposed to be drawing attention to ourselves,' Arnie said as they climbed the narrow staircase to their bedroom.

'I wasn't drawing attention,' said Chas. 'I was preparing an alibi. Dad always said, make sure you've got an alibi.'

'Saying you were fast asleep isn't much of an alibi,'

grunted Arnie. 'And anyway, I thought nothing could possibly go wrong.'

They were in their room now. Chas hung the DO NOT DISTURB notice on the outside of the door, then locked it behind them. He banged his head on the low ceiling beam, drew the curtains and peered under the bed to make sure nobody was there. He checked the walls for electronic bugs, banging his head again, then spread a map out on the bed.

'Right,' he said at last, pretending his head didn't hurt. 'This is a plan of the dinosaur museum.' He pointed at the map. 'This is the window you will break into.'

Arnie nodded. Breaking into places wasn't usually a problem.

'This is the door you will open from the inside to let me in.'

Arnie nodded again. No problem there.

'And this is the laboratory that contains the item we are about to, er, liberate.'

Arnie nodded again. 'What about alarms?' he said. 'On the windows and doors.'

Chas flicked open a notebook. 'I've checked those

out from photos. Looks like they're the old-fashioned G42A type.'

'Piece of cake,' said Arnie, then wished he hadn't, as it reminded him of the chocolate and fudge gateau he'd just missed out on.

'And this . . .' Chas took a large padded bag from his suitcase, 'is what you will place the item in once you have removed it from the laboratory.'

Arnie looked from the bag to Chas. 'So are you finally gonna tell me what it is that I'm supposed to be nicking?'

'An egg,' said Chas. He held himself upright, avoiding the ceiling beam. 'A dinosaur's egg.'

There was a moment's silence, then Arnie laughed.

'You're winding me up. Dinosaurs don't lay eggs.'

Chas looked annoyed. 'Course they do. Did,' he said. He took a sheet of printed paper from his breast pocket. 'And this isn't any old bog-standard egg.' He unfolded the paper. 'This information was posted on the dinosaur museum website twelve hours ago. A mega mistake, obviously. It was taken down again sharpish but not before I'd spotted it. Chas pointed triumphantly at the words on the paper.

Recent finds: Egg. Probably
Neovenator Salerii.
Status: Complete. Fossilised.
Condition: Remarkably good.
Possibly intact embryo.
Action: Investigate for traces
of living DNA . . .

Chas looked at Arnie, his eyes shining. 'D'you see what I'm getting at?'

Arnie sat heavily on his bed. He shook his head. 'No.'

'They're looking for DNA, Arnie. They think there could be living DNA. And if they can extract DNA, what could they do then?'

Arnie shrugged. He didn't know or care.

'They could grow a dinosaur,' cried Chas. 'A *real* dinosaur. One with teeth and claws and scaly skin. Real. Alive!'

Arnie shrugged again. 'OK, I can see that's interesting for those who like that sort of thing. But what do you want a dinosaur for? You live in a tiny flat in London.'

Chas put his face close to Arnie's.

'I don't want it for myself, bonebrain. But there are collectors who would. People with money. Shedloads of money. They'll fight each other to pay a fortune for the egg.'

Arnie considered this for a moment.

'Right,' he said. 'I see. But how are you going to let them know you've got it?'

'Easy,' beamed Chas. 'I'll advertise it on eBay.'

4
The Break-In

While Chas and Arnie Thickett were planning their crime of the century, and the sheep were snoring peacefully, Tod and Ida were enjoying themselves only a few miles away near the seaside town of Ventnor. They were in a huge shed in the grounds of Headland Manor and they were admiring a huge trailer attached to a huge tractor. Rex Headland and the rest of the carnival committee were there too, and they were all as excited as each other.

'Wow,' said Ida, 'that's what I call a trailer.'

Rex beamed. 'Glad you like it, dear lady. I'm determined that this year's carnival will be the biggest and best ever.' He lowered his voice. 'To be frank, last year's float wasn't up to scratch. Organisation was a bit shambolic. No discipline in the ranks, you see. But with a bit of military precision, and your help, of course, I'm sure that this time around we can show the world what we're really made of.'

Rex, who had recently celebrated his sixtieth birthday, was tall and slim with a sun-tanned face and thick white hair. He had served in the army when he was younger and still walked and talked like an officer. Headlands had lived at Headland Manor since 1575 and Rex was very proud of his heritage. He saw it as his duty to take care of the local people and supported all their events, especially the carnival.

Tod walked slowly around the trailer. It was simply a long, flat base, supported on three sets of wheels. It was massive. It was ideal. They could build anything on top of it if they had the materials and manpower. He imagined it supporting a medieval castle, or a pirate ship or a space rocket. He glanced over at Gran. She still hadn't told him what she had up her sleeve, but as he watched her she caught his eye and gave him a slow wink. She wasn't going to say anything yet.

'Well, what do you think, young man?' asked Rex, tapping the trailer with his furled umbrella.

'The trailer's perfect,' said Tod. 'But we'll need loads of help.'

'And help you shall have.' Rex nodded at the other men and women standing around the trailer. 'No shortage of willing manpower in this army.'

There was a chorus of cheerful agreement.

Ida clambered on to the trailer and put her hands on her hips.

'Right then,' she called. 'Down to business. Any carpenters here?'

Two men raised their hands.

'Good,' said Ida. 'You're going to be *very* busy. Any painters?'

Four people raised their hands.

'Good. Electricians?

One man raised his hand.

'We need more than one,' said Ida. 'I'm planning some very exciting lighting effects.

The electrician promised to get a couple more to help him.

'Dressmakers? We're going to need a whole team of people who can cut and sew fabric.'

Plenty of people volunteered for this task.

'Anyone know about sound systems?'

'Sound systems?' Rex raised his bushy eyebrows in

surprise. 'Do we need a sound system?'

'We certainly do,' said Ida. 'Two in fact. One for the music and one for the sound effects.'

'Sound effects?' Rex's bushy eyebrows rose even higher, almost meeting his thick white hair.

'Oh, yes,' said Ida, enjoying playing everyone along. 'Now, what else . . .?'

'Someone to drive the Land Rover, Gran,' Tod reminded her.

'That'll be me,' said Fred Jolliff, who was standing at the back of the crowd. 'I be too busy with the farm to do much else but I'll be happy to drive on the night.'

'Thanks, Fred,' said Rex. He turned to Ida. 'Well, dear lady. We're all agog. Are you going to tell us exactly what you've got planned?'

Ida nodded slowly, looking around the shed. 'Yes . . .' she said. 'But first, I'm going to swear you all to secrecy.'

Tod smiled a little smile. Gran always did this. Keeping the plan secret was half the fun.

'Cross your carnival heart,' said Ida.

Rex laughed out loud. 'Wonderful, my dear. The element of surprise is most important on any mission.'

He tucked his furled umbrella under his arm. 'I propose we all take an oath of secrecy. Ida's the word.'

'Ida's the word,' laughed everyone else, hands on hearts.

And satisfied that they were all keen to keep the secret, Ida leaned forward and told her eager listeners how she intended to transform the trailer into the most amazing carnival float the Island had ever seen.

Fred Jolliff hurried away as soon as the meeting was over.

'G'night now,' he called to Ida and Tod as he drove away. 'And don't you worry 'bout they little sheep o'yourn. They'll be sleeping like lambs.'

The five sheep on holiday from Eppingham Farm were indeed deep in slumber. But not in Penny Pasture. Fred drove past The Dragon's Nest on his way home from Ventnor. He didn't see the five white lumps by the hedge, not even when one of them moved. Links had been woken by the headlights. He yawned and shook the curls from his eyes. Wills was next to him, snuggled close to Sal, and Links remembered how upset the lamb had been for bringing them to a pub instead of to a proper dragon's nest.

'The little guy needs a rap, innit?' Links said softly to himself. 'Cool and sweet to build him up again for the mornin'.' He began to nod and slowly the words came:

'Now Willsy man, you is the coolest lamb,
Remember how you led us to Aries the Ram?
How you got us out West, where Red Tongue
    was king,
How we brought him down,
Took the shine off his bling?
How we followed our Destiny right Down Under,
And you led us all the way to the Final Thunder . . .?'

He was working on a rhyme for Dragon's Nest when another light briefly intruded on the darkness. Not a car's headlamps this time. There hadn't been any other traffic since Fred had passed by. This was just a thin horizontal band of light high up on the side of the pub. Links looked up. The band of light widened a little. He heard a faint creaking sound, a human voice, whispering urgently, then nothing. Links watched for a few moments, then went back to composing his rap. Except that his head was no longer nodding with the beat. It was nodding with returning sleep.

So Wills, don't beat yourself up 'bout no Dragon's
    Nest,
You's our *go*-to-guy. The Best of the Best . . .'

His last line ended in a snore.

Up in their bedroom, Chas and Arnie were experiencing a spot of unexpected bother. The room was fitted with sash windows, the sort you push up to open. Arnie had pushed it up enough for him to get one leg out. He'd felt around with his dangling foot and found the edge of a drainpipe. So far so good. He only had to get the rest of himself through the window, then shin down the pipe. But the window wouldn't budge another inch and Arnie was stuck half in and half out.

'Careful!' he whispered at Chas, who was inside the room, straining to push the window upwards. 'You're shoving me out!'

Chas climbed on to a chair and got his shoulder under the window frame.

'Stupid old-fashioned place,' he muttered. 'Why don't they get rid of these and install electronic windows?'

'Why don't we just walk downstairs?' retorted Arnie.

'Because we don't want to draw attention to ourselves,' replied Chas through gritted teeth.

He took a deep breath and heaved upwards against the bottom of the window. The frame creaked, wiggled a bit and then suddenly shot right up. Chas lost his balance and toppled forward from the chair. His head hit Arnie's stomach and Arnie did an inelegant backwards somersault from the window sill. Miraculously, he landed feet first on the lawn, but was instantly flattened as Chas plummeted down on top of him. They lay in a tangled heap for a moment.

'You alive?' asked Arnie.

'Sshhh . . .' hissed Chas.

'Anything broken?'

'Sshhh! No, I don't think so.'

They got painfully to their feet.

'If anyone comes, we were studying the stars

when we fell,' whispered Chas.

They stood for a moment, trying to look as if falling out of a window while studying the stars was perfectly normal. And as if being dressed in black tracksuits, soft black running shoes, with black scarves around their faces, and head torches on top, was also perfectly normal in the middle of the night. But nobody came. Not a sound broke the silence, except for the snores of the five sheep sleeping against the hedge.

'Let's go,' whispered Chas, and he limped away, out of the car park and across the road.

The dinosaur museum was a large, old-fashioned brick building with small windows and a narrow front entrance. Arnie thought it looked a bit like a prison. They crept around to the back of the building then stood listening. Nothing. Still silence. Arnie looked up at the tiny window he was supposed to climb through.

'Well, what are you waiting for?' Chas whispered. He bent his knees and braced his feet firmly on the ground. 'Go for it.'

Arnie swung himself up on to his brother's shoulders and from there reached up to the window sill. He hauled himself up on to it and paused for a moment to get his balance. The burglar alarm was fixed to the wall just to the side of the window. He took a pair of wire cutters from the soft leather tool bag belted around his waist and deftly snipped at the pathetic G42A alarm. The feeble little green light went out as Arnie disconnected it. Arnie paused for a moment, remembering what his dad had taught him. 'Take your time, Son. Never hurry, never worry.' He carefully wrapped a cloth from his tool bag around his fist, then, with one swift movement, punched a hole through the window pane. He paused again. But the cloth had deadened the sound of shattering glass. Again nobody came running to investigate. Arnie reached through the hole, being careful not to cut himself, fiddled with the catch for a moment, then swung the window open and climbed through.

'*That's* the way to do it,' he said, and dropped softly to the floor inside the museum.

He switched on his head torch. The narrow beam of light shone sideways, picking out a life-sized and very realistic crocodile. Arnie jumped, then adjusted his torch, which had twisted round when he landed. Now the beam of light shone on a glass case full of bones and stones. 'What do people see in all this stuff?' he muttered to himself as he padded softly towards the back door. It had a simple lock. No bolts. Arnie carefully opened the door a crack and Chas slipped through and shut it behind him.

'What d'you think you're doing?' said Arnie, opening the door again. '*Never* close doors behind you. Always know your exit route. Dad's been telling us that since we could walk.'

'Yeah, yeah, yeah,' whispered Chas, annoyed that Arnie was telling *him* what Dad always said. 'Now, where's the laboratory?' He glanced at his little map of the museum. 'Ah, here. Past the crocodiles and the Iguanadon . . .'

Chas crept slowly along, following the tiny beam of light from his head torch. Arnie followed. Away from the crocodile.

'What's that smell?' asked Arnie, wrinkling his nose.

'Primeval swamp. They pump the smell into the air to show you what it was like millions of years ago.'

'Oh,' said Arnie. 'Thought it might be your socks.'

'Will you shut up.'

Chas glanced at his map again. The laboratory

should be just to his right. His heart thumped. He was only inches away from getting his hands on a fortune. Forget winning the lottery. This was going to be way bigger. But before he could take another step, Arnie grabbed his shoulder and pulled him backwards.

Arnie clamped his hand over Chas's mouth to prevent him speaking. He dragged his brother back a few steps more and forced him to crouch down behind a case full of dinosaur skulls. He switched off both their head torches. They hunched there for a moment, tense and silent. Then they both heard what Arnie's sharp ears had picked up. Soft footsteps.

The footsteps came closer and closer. They stopped a few paces in front and to the right of the brothers. One of the overhead lights flicked on. Arnie tensed his body, ready to charge for the exit, but Chas put a restraining hand on his arm. The light was quickly dimmed, but they could now see the owner of the footsteps: a young woman, standing by the laboratory door. Unlike the rest of the museum, the laboratory was sleek and modern with glass walls so that visitors could watch the scientists and craftsmen at work. It had a large glass door, which the woman slid silently aside. She took a bunch of keys from her denim skirt pocket and opened the small glass specimen case which stood on a workbench in the middle of the room.

Chas watched open-mouthed as the woman leaned into the case and took out a yellowish grey egg, the size of a small football. The dinosaur egg. *His* egg. She slipped it carefully into the capacious pink duffel bag she had brought with her.

Arnie noticed that she was wearing cotton gloves. He nodded approvingly. Good practice.

The woman locked the case and slipped the keys back into her pocket. Then she paused and drew a deep breath. Arnie and Chas held theirs. The young woman took a small hammer from a rack of tools. She raised it above her head, then smashed the glass front of the case. She glanced round anxiously, picked up her pink bag, switched off the light and headed for the rear exit.

Once again, Arnie was impressed. 'Nice one,' he whispered. 'Must be an employee trying to make it look like an outside job.'

The young woman, treading very softly despite

her heavy lace-up boots, passed right by the brothers' hiding place. At the back door she stood for a moment. Mission accomplished.

That was when Chas wrenched himself free of Arnie's grip.

'Oi, where d'you think you're going with that egg?' he shouted, racing towards the young woman.

She turned and saw Chas coming at her, his eyes blazing in the darkness. The next moment he was lunging at her pink bag, trying to prise it out of her hand. But she was slim, fit and several inches taller than Chas. She pushed him away, then jerked her arm upwards. The bag with its precious dinosaur egg dangled above his head. Chas slammed the door to prevent the woman's escape, then jumped up and down, trying to grab the bag from her hand. The young woman backed away but held tight to her pink bag, fending off Chas with her other arm.

'Thief!' Chas shouted. 'Burglar!'

Arnie strode towards his yo-yoing brother. 'Brilliant,' he muttered, sarcastically. 'Very subtle, bruv.'

But just as he reached the struggling pair, the young woman dodged away. She stumbled against a showcase full of tiny bones. Some of them must have been very special because the case itself was alarmed and as the woman crashed into it, a high pitched wail tore the air. And went on tearing it.

Arnie jumped, winced, then started to run. He grabbed Chas's arm as he passed him and kept on running, dragging his brother along with him, out of the back door. The woman had picked herself up and got there before them. She disappeared into the darkness.

Across the road in the pub garden, the five slumbering sheep were woken with a fright.

'Whassat?' grunted Oxo, struggling to his feet.

The others stood up and gathered around him. They had no idea what was making the noise but they knew it hurt their ears and set their nerves on edge.

'Ohmygrass . . .' cried Jaycey. 'Ohmyears . . .'

Oxo took the lead. 'Follow me,' he said sternly. Though he had no idea where to. He marched across the garden and into the car park in front of the pub. Then stopped at the entrance while the others clustered around him. They stood very still in the darkness, waiting for Oxo to tell them what to do next.

Luckily, he didn't have to think. Without warning, two human figures hurtled towards them from across the road. Whump! Arnie and Chas charged straight into the little group of sheep.

For the second time that night, the brothers crashed to the ground. Arnie, being the more athletic of the two, turned his fall into a forward roll. Chas would have splatted face first on to the tarmac if Sal hadn't been there. He grabbed hold of her fleece as he went down and only the tip of his nose was grazed. Sal bucked sideways to shake off the human clutching at her fleece. She began bleating loudly in fright. The others were also bleating in panic as they ran this way and that, not knowing what had happened

'Ohmygrass . . .' squealed Jaycey. 'Is it a dragon, Sal? Is it a *dragon*?'

Sal didn't answer. She was staggering around in a circle, dazed by the collision.

The humans stumbled to their feet and headed for the garden. Arnie scrambled up the drainpipe like the professional burglar he was and dropped quietly back into their room. He pulled a sheet from his bed, hung it out of the window and hauled Chas up.

'She's nicked my egg . . .' Chas moaned as his knees bounced off the brick wall. 'My baby monster in a shell; my passport to riches. She's nicked it!'

A small, frightened lamb in the garden below heard his words. 'Nicked it. She's nicked it.' Wills was sure he'd heard that word before. It was ringing alarm bells in his head as loud as the alarm still shrieking inside the museum. If only he could remember what it meant.

5
Nicked

The siren in the museum was soon joined by another. This one blaring from a police car as it raced towards the scene of the crime.

Lights came on in the pub and the landlady appeared in the doorway, her hands clamped over her ears. The first thing she saw was a bunch of terrified sheep, galloping this way and that around her car park. The little flock finally came together then, as one, baaed and galloped away round the side of the building. The landlady stared after them, wondering if she was dreaming. And then wondering if her guests were still asleep? She'd told them it was quiet as the grave here at night. Some grave!

The police car screeched to a halt. Its siren was shut down and four policemen leapt out of the car. One checked the front door to the museum and the other three hurried around to the back. A few moments later the security alarm stopped mid-shriek. The pub landlady took her hands from her ears.

What a relief! she thought.

Up in their room, Arnie and Chas were scrambling out of their black burglary outfits and into pyjamas. Arnie dived into his bed and pulled the duvet over his head. Chas clambered into his, still muttering, 'How dare she nick my egg? How dare she?'

Down below, in the garden, the sheep were once more huddled against the hedge. The terrifying noise had stopped but they were all still shaking.

'We's supposed to be the Warrior Sheep, innit?' said Links, pulling himself together. 'But we well let ourselves down there. Runnin' around like a bunch o' silly chickens.'

'We can't help our instincts, dear,' said Sal. 'In times of danger, sheep flee. Even Rare Breeds.' She sat down with a soft thump of fleece against grass. 'It aids survival and therefore *is* the sensible thing to do. Just another example of why we are renowned for our cunning and resourcefulness.'

'Right,' agreed Oxo. 'And I'm renowned for eating. Getting scared makes you hungry.' He buried his nose in the lawn and started to chomp. A few mouthfuls later he looked up. 'I don't hear anyone being cunning or resourcewhatsit.'

Links tossed the curls out of his eyes. 'Over to you, man,' he said, looking at Wills. 'That's your department.'

Wills dropped his head and looked at his hooves.

'Erm . . .'

'Spit it out,' mumbled Oxo through a mouthful of grass.

'Well . . .' said Wills. 'One of those men who bashed into us said something about an egg.'

'What egg?' Blades of soggy grass dropped from Oxo's mouth on to Jaycey's back.

'Oh, purleeze . . .' she said, shaking them off disgustedly.

Wills began to feel a little braver. 'I don't know. But his exact words were: "My baby monster in a shell; my passport to riches. She's nicked it!"'

For a moment nobody spoke, then Links said, 'A baby monster in a shell? That's gotta be a dragon, innit?'

Wills shrugged. He was still worried about being wrong again. 'The thing is, I've been trying and trying and I've just remembered what the word *nicked* means.'

'And? What does it mean?' More soggy grass stalks dropped from Oxo's lips.

'Ida used it in spring when you were all being sheared,' said Wills, slowly.

He was too young to have been sheared himself but he had watched Ida shear the others. She had grabbed them one by one, turned them upside down, then swiftly run a pair of electric clippers all over their bodies. It only took a minute or two.

They'd all said that it wasn't nice while it was happening but worth it as they felt so cool and clean afterwards.

'If you remember, Sal,' said Wills, 'Ida cut you a tiny bit behind the ear.'

'Did she?' said Sal. 'No, I don't remember but go on.'

'Well, she did and she looked upset and she said . . . "Oh, dear, Sal. I've nicked you."'

There was silence while the others thought about this.

Then Links said, 'So nicking is like . . . cutting?'

Wills nodded. 'I think so.'

'Ohymgrass . . .' cried Jaycey. 'If the shell's been nicked, the baby dragons'll soon come out and fill the sky!'

'Exactly,' said Sal, heaving herself to her feet. 'Just what I've been thinking all along.'

They'd all seen chicks hatching in the barn. A tiny crack in the egg shell got larger and larger, and finally a chick's head struggled through the hole.

'They're probably pecking their way out as we speak,' said Sal. 'We haven't a moment to lose.' She stood poised for a moment then, realising that it was still dark, she sat down again. 'We set off at the crack of egg!' she declared.

It was way past the crack of egg or even the crack of dawn when the Warriors finally woke up again. They had a quick snack of lawn then hurried round to the car park. Chas and Arnie were already there. They were standing by their van, pretending to study their Isle of Wight map, but they were really looking at the museum across the road. And the police car which was still there. They didn't notice the arrival of the sheep they'd fallen over the night before.

'Why don't we buy a ticket and go inside to see what's going on?' Arnie asked grumpily. He was fed up because he was starving and Chas hadn't let him have breakfast. 'We're supposed to be tourists, aren't we?'

'It won't be open yet, will it. Anyway, never revisit the scene of your crime,' said Chas primly. 'Dad always said . . .' He didn't finish the sentence. A young woman had just cycled into the museum car park opposite. She dismounted close to the police car, took off her helmet and shook out a mop of thick, dark hair.

'That's her!' cried Chas. 'The woman who nicked my egg!'

'Not so loud!' Arnie glanced around. He noticed the sheep for the first time. And especially he noticed the skinny lamb. It was staring as if taking in every word. It turned to the others and baaed and they all trotted briskly away across the road towards the museum. For a moment, Arnie actually wondered if the animal *had* heard. And understood. He shook his head. Lack of breakfast always affected his brain.

The Warriors stopped close to the dark-haired

young woman. The one they were now certain had nicked the egg. Hadn't one of the men just said so?

The woman glanced at them once but took no more notice. She wasn't interested in a bunch of sheep. She moved away quickly towards a uniformed policeman who was searching the car park. He'd been on duty all night and was tired and irritable.

'What's going on?' she asked him. 'What are you looking for?'

The policeman bent down to peer under the hedge. 'Go inside, please,' he said. 'Your boss'll tell you.'

The dark-haired woman nipped between the policeman and a line of wheelie bins ranged against the side wall.

'Have we been burgled?' she asked. 'Or should I say baaaargled?' She laughed at her own joke and pointed at the little group of sheep.

The policeman sighed. 'Please go inside, Miss,' he said, shooing her towards the front door. He followed her into the museum. He forgot to lift the lids and look inside the wheelie bins.

The Warriors trotted swiftly towards the door but the policeman shut it before they got there. 'Baaargled . . .'

he said, raising his eyebrows. 'Ho woolly ho.'

There was nothing else the sheep could do but settle down to watch and wait.

And in the pub car park opposite, Chas and Arnie had no choice either. They stood beside their van, still pretending to be studying their map. Even though it was upside down.

Inside the museum, Denzil Adams the curator, a short, slim, nervous man with grey hair and dirty fingernails, was preparing to address his staff. He would much rather have been on the beach, hunting for fossils. He glanced up when the dark-haired woman came in.

'Hello, Candy,' he said. 'Right, we're all here now, so I'll begin. It's quite simple really. Someone broke in last night and stole our latest and most prized and secret find. The Neovenator egg.'

There were gasps of shock and horror from the little group of men and women.

Mr Adams continued, 'The police have searched the museum from top to bottom but found nothing. So it looks as if the burglar or burglars – there were probably more than one of them – have got clean away with it.' He shuddered. 'I can't bear to think of the possible consequences.'

Nods and mutters of agreement replaced the gasps of shock and horror.

A plain clothes CID officer flicked his notebook open. The smell of bacon cooking in the pub across the road was making his stomach rumble.

'OK,' he said, 'if we've got no leads on *how* this egg was stolen, let's turn to the motive. *Why* was it stolen?'

The staff looked down and shuffled their feet. Nobody wanted to speak. The policeman glared at them then carried on.

'Mr Adams tells me that nobody apart from yourselves even knew it was here.' He paused. 'So are we looking at an inside job? Is one of you the culprit?'

More shuffling of feet, then Mr Adams clasped his hands together and spoke. 'I'm afraid it's not strictly true that nobody else could have known.' He looked bravely at the CID officer. 'It's all my fault. In my excitement, I actually listed the egg amongst the Recent Finds data on our website.'

'I see . . .' said the CID officer coolly.

'It was out there for several hours before I realised

my mistake and took it down.'

'I see,' said the CID officer icily.

'Don't beat yourself up about it, Mr Adams,' said the dark-haired woman, Candy. She smiled warmly at him. 'It's easily done. We've all pressed the wrong button at some time or other.'

Mr Adams managed a miserable smile. 'Thank you, Candy, but –'

'OK,' said the CID officer. 'So the top secret news isn't entirely top secret. What exactly are the consequences you're so worried about?'

Mr Adams tried to speak but his voice had dried up. Candy helped him out.

'We believe there might just be a chance that the egg contains some live DNA. Some cells that could possibly be grown on in a suitably equipped laboratory. And that a living dinosaur could be incubated.'

The CID officer stared hard at her. 'Right . . .' he said. He was beginning to think this was an enormous wind-up. 'So you reckon someone out there's going to use stuff from this egg to grow monsters?'

Candy nodded. 'It's just possible.'

The CID officer snapped his notebook shut. 'I see.

Well, we'll do our best to locate your egg, of course, but as I'm sure you'll appreciate, we are rather busy just now. What with carnivals and sandcastle competitions . . .'

He nodded briskly at his uniformed colleagues, turned on his heel and stalked away. The uniforms stalked after him.

Mr Adams looked wildly round at his staff, then ran after the policemen. 'But, Officer. This could be *the* biggest crime you'll ever have to deal with!'

The CID officer wasn't listening. He got into his car and slammed the door. 'This is the Isle of Wight,' he muttered, 'not Jurassic Park.'

As Mr Adams trailed back to the museum and his worried staff, he was watched by seven pairs of eyes. Five pairs, the yellow ones, belonged to the little huddle of sheep standing just outside the museum front door. The other two pairs, hidden behind dark glasses, belonged to Chas and Arnie, still standing beside their van with their upside-down map.

Inside the museum, Mr Adams plonked himself on a chair and put his head in his hands. 'They're not taking us seriously,' he groaned.

There was an uncomfortable silence. Then Candy spoke.

'I could have a go at finding it. At least I know what it looks like.'

Mr Adams looked up. 'No, Candy. I can't let you do that. We have no idea who took it. They might be dangerous.'

Candy shrugged. 'I can take care of myself. Just give me a few days off and I'll see what I can do.'

Mr Adams looked at Candy's heavy lace-up boots and strong wrists and suddenly felt a spark of hope.

A few minutes later, Candy Fenton was marching out of the main door of the museum, a broad grin on her face and a bounce in her step. She strode to the bicycle rack and unlocked her bike. Then, glancing around, she lifted the lid of a green wheelie bin and drew out the pink bag she'd hidden there the night before. Looking around again, she carefully took out the dinosaur egg, inspected it quickly then popped it back into her pink bag. She slung the bag across her shoulder and mounted her bike.

'She's got an egg in the bag, innit!' cried Links excitedly. 'A ginormous egg.'

'Ohmygrass . . .' said Jaycey. 'What do we do now?'

'Follow me,' shouted Oxo. 'Five for one and one for the crusher!'

The little flock trotted quickly out on to the road and were right behind Candy when she pedalled off.

Chas and Arnie weren't so quick. Especially Arnie.

'Clever girl,' he'd said approvingly as he watched the dark-haired girl take the bag from the wheelie bin. 'Nice little hiding place.'

Chas was already panicking. He dropped the map and jumped into the van.

'Give me the keys. Quick!' he called.

'I haven't got them, you have,' said Arnie.

Chas jumped out again and they stood beside the van, glaring at each other.

'They must be in one of your pockets,' Arnie said.

Chas had given up on the tweed jacket and, despite the warm day, was wearing a hoodie adorned with several dozen useful zip pockets. He began frantically patting pockets and unzipping zips. Arnie snorted, then lifted his racing bike from the van.

'See you when I see you, bruv,' he called as he pedalled out of the car park.

Candy cycled fast from the museum to the nearby crossroads and then on to the main road that led to Sandy Bay. She didn't look back once. The Warriors were galloping behind her. Arnie had no choice but to ride behind *them*. He bent low over his handlebars, muttering and occasionally shouting at the sheep.

From the museum to Sandy Bay wasn't far for a cyclist to pedal but it was a long way for a sheep to run, especially a rather fat one like Sal.

'You'll have to go on without me, dears,' she puffed as they reached the town centre.

'Just a bit more, Sal,' called Wills. 'Look. She's slowing down.'

He was right. Candy was having to weave through a crowd. The town was busy with holidaymakers in shorts and T-shirts. They were strolling about, licking ice creams, taking photographs, and wandering in and out of the road. Most were heading for the beach.

Hundreds of little flags hung on strings across the streets and a large sign announced:

GRAND SANDCASTLE COMPETITION

TODAY!

PRIZES FOR THE BEST

Candy stopped in a side street near the beach and chained her bike to a tree. She didn't notice five sheep gallop into the street behind her, even though they skidded to a halt, puffing and panting just a few yards away. Nor did she notice the cyclist who whizzed in after the sheep. Nor the van marked MR FIXALL which screeched up after the cyclist. Candy was on a mission. She patted the pink duffel bag on her shoulder and strode away towards the beach.

The sheep and Chas and Arnie followed.

'Shouldn't they have a shepherd or something with them?' asked Chas, glaring at the little flock.

Candy stopped when she got to the beach and glanced left and right. It was a long expanse but today it was crammed with people of all ages intently building sandcastles. Some were digging; some were piling sand and patting it into shape. Others were running back and forwards with plastic buckets full of seawater to soften the sand. Others still were collecting shells and feathers and seaweed to decorate their creations.

Candy picked her way through the busy builders and their castles until she found a clear space, then sat carefully in an empty deckchair. She glanced at her watch and settled back, clutching her pink bag on her lap. The sheep gathered on the promenade just a few feet above her head.

'Ohmygrass . . .' said Jaycey. 'We don't have to get down on to that *sand* stuff, do we? It sooooo scratches my hooves.'

'Hard to walk on too, innit?' said Links. 'Unless you's one o' them humpy things.'

'You mean camels?' asked Wills.

'Do I?' said Links.

'Sshhh, dears.' Sal sat down on the concrete promenade. 'We must be patient. When the moment's right, we will spring into action and snatch the dragon's egg.'

Wills wasn't sure how, being sheep, they could do much snatching but he didn't say so.

'Unless she nicks it again,' said Oxo. 'In which case, we're goin' in hard.'

The Warriors settled down to watch. Their yellow eyes unblinking.

Chas and Arnie were also watching the woman with the pink bag. They were standing on the sand just a few paces away from her deckchair.

'What if she recognises us?' whispered Arnie.

'She won't,' Chas whispered back. 'It was dark. And our faces were covered.'

The woman glanced up and saw them.

'You looking for someone?' she asked politely.

'No,' said Chas.

'Yes,' said Arnie.

'Not *someone*,' said Chas, digging Arnie in the ribs. 'We were . . . just looking for a good spot to er, um . . .'

'Build a sandcastle,' Arnie finished the sentence.

Candy smiled. 'Go a bit closer to the sea,' she said. 'The sand's firmer there.'

'Thanks,' said Arnie with a grin.

The brothers moved away a bit.

'Great!' said Chas with a scowl as he plonked himself down on the sand. 'Building sandcastles. What could be better?'

But Arnie was already scraping.

Ten minutes passed. Candy fidgeted nervously but remained sitting in her deckchair. Occasionally she glanced over at the two young men sitting on the damp sand nearby.

'Why don't we just rush her?' asked Arnie, looking up from his mound of sand.

Chas glanced at the woman's heavy lace-up boots. One of those could give a nasty kick.

'No . . .' he said, 'too many people about.'

'In that case,' said Arnie, 'I'll get on with this.' He got up and strolled away. A few minutes later he returned with a couple of buckets and spades.

'Where d'you get those?' Chas asked.

'A kid along the beach,' said Arnie. 'He's swimming. Won't miss them for a bit.' He started building in earnest.

More people arrived on the beach and settled themselves in the space between the brothers and the woman with the pink bag. Chas sighed and wished they'd rushed her while they had the chance. It was too late now.

Arnie's sandcastle, a large square block, was almost

complete. He began carefully pressing ice-lolly sticks on to the sides to look like barred windows.

'That's not much of a castle,' said Chas scornfully. 'It looks more like a prison.'

'It is a prison,' Arnie replied. 'Brixton. I know it well.' He glanced round at the sandcastles nearby. 'I reckon I'm in with a chance of winning,' he said, pleased with himself.

Chas sighed again and returned to observing the woman in the deckchair. Was she going to sit there all day? The Warriors were beginning to wonder the same. They were getting a lot of attention, perched on the promenade.

Then suddenly a woman carrying a bulging plastic carrier bag came and sat on the wall beside them. She was wearing a sundress, a white linen jacket, an orange baseball cap that completely shaded her face and huge sunglasses. She took a mobile phone from her pocket.

Seconds later, the phone in Candy's bag rang. She fumbled for it, listened for a moment then stood up.

She placed the pink bag carefully on her deckchair and walked away.

6
Sandcastles

For a moment the Warriors were too astonished to move.

Chas and Arnie were too. The final lolly stick that Arnie was about to press on to his prison fell from his fingers. He stared at the pink bag sitting innocently on the deckchair. 'It's a swap,' he breathed. 'Quick!'

But as he scrambled to his feet, the woman sitting on the promenade next to the sheep slid from the wall down on to the sand. She strolled casually to the deckchair and picked up the pink bag.

Thirty paces further along the beach, Candy had stopped and turned. She watched, poised. Ready to race back if the woman in the huge sunglasses tried to cheat her. Candy didn't know the woman's name or anything else about her. Except that she wanted the dinosaur egg badly and was prepared to pay a huge sum of money for it.

The woman lifted her sunglasses slightly and peeked into Candy's pink bag. The egg was there. She glanced up. Candy was waiting along the beach, exactly as she'd been told to. Without making any fuss, the woman hitched the pink bag on to her shoulder and placed her plastic carrier bag on the deckchair in its place. She raised her hand in a little wave at Candy, then turned to go. Her eyes, hidden behind the enormous sunglasses, twinkled.

This was *so* easy.

She didn't hear the baaas behind her as five sheep launched themselves from the promenade on to the beach.

'Ohmygrass . . .' cried Jaycey as her hooves sank into the soft, hot sand between the promenade wall and the deckchair. 'Ohmyhooves . . .'

'We's the Warrior Sheep an' we won't be beat!' cried Links as he and Sal thumped on to the beach next to Jaycey.

Oxo rather overdid it. His leap took him right over the top of the deckchair.

'Egg nicker . . .!' he yelled as he shot over the

79

startled woman standing beside it.

He produced a great shower of gritty sand as he landed. Most of it hit the faces of the two men who were racing up the beach towards the deckchair, dodging sandcastles at they ran. They staggered backwards and fell over, scrabbled upright, then ploughed up the beach again.

'Death to the dragons!' shouted Wills, who was still on the promenade, bouncing up and down. A final bounce sprang him from the wall on to the deckchair and his weight catapulted the plastic bag into the air. It thudded down again on the sand, splitting slightly as it landed. A few ten pound notes slipped out of the hole and fluttered away in the light sea breeze.

Sunglass Woman was suddenly flustered. She stooped and grabbed up the bulging plastic carrier bag containing the rest of her money. But as she did so, the pink bag slipped from her shoulder. Before she could retrieve it, something shoved her from behind. Hard. She fell flat on her face in the soft sand.

'Ohmygrass . . .!' Jaycey cried. 'Stop, Links. Stop! Don't butt her again. She might roll on the egg and crack it!'

'Jacey, man, that is the whole point!' grunted Links, winding up for another charge. 'We's stoppin' the dragons before they gets started, innit.'

Sunglass Woman floundered to her knees, wondering what on earth had hit her. She wiped the sand from her sunglasses and peered through them. There seemed to be several causes. All of them sheep. And the biggest of all, a huge ram, was now bulldozing up the beach towards her. Close behind the ram, two men coated in gritty sand were also racing her way. She gulped. Then, from the corner of her eye, she saw Candy tearing back along the beach, leaping over sandcastles as she came. Sunglass Woman leaned on the side of the deckchair and hauled herself upright. That's when the bouncing lamb pinged off and hit her in the stomach with its sharp little horns. She crumpled to her knees again.

Before he could get in another butt, Wills felt a black leather boot slide under his tummy. It lifted him off his feet and tossed him aside. Candy reached down, snatched up her pink bag with its precious dinosaur egg, and ran.

Oxo saw her go. He veered sharply to his left,

charging after Candy as she made her escape. Wills sprang to his hooves and followed Oxo. The others joined the chase.

'One for five and five for the egg nicker!' yelled Oxo, as the Warriors galloped after the woman with the pink bag.

Behind them, Sunglass Woman finally staggered to her feet, gasping and shaking. A few more ten pound notes fluttered from the carrier bag she was clutching to her chest. Curious holidaymakers caught them and tried to hand them back but the woman just pulled her baseball cap even lower over her face and hurried away. In the opposite direction.

Meanwhile, Candy careered along the beach. She hurdled some sandcastles, skidded round some more and ploughed straight through the middle of others. Those that she didn't tread on were trampled by the pursuing sheep. Artistic fairy castles collapsed. Cars, boats, planes, dinosaurs and all sorts of other wonderful sand sculptures were flattened. Shells, little flags and trails of seaweed were tossed in every direction. Children cried and angry adults shouted and raced after the castle spoilers.

Candy went on running. She exploded past two men at the end of the beach who had just begun judging the competition. They gasped and stared open-mouthed at the sheep, angry, chasing holidaymakers and trail of destruction.

'Vandal!' one of them shouted at Candy. 'Heartless vandal!'

Candy didn't hear. She leapt on to the promenade and sprinted to where she'd left her bicycle. Moments later, she was pedalling furiously away into the maze of side streets, the pink bag slung securely across her chest.

Oxo, Links, Wills and Jaycey skidded to a halt. There was no way they could catch the woman now.

'She's got away, innit?' panted Links. 'We need wheels, man. We's never gonna catch her on hooves. We's never gonna get the dragon's egg from her now!'

Sal puffed up and the five Warriors stood dejectedly on the pavement. Oxo had a trail of seaweed dangling over one eye. He poked out his tongue and tried it for taste.

'Mmm. Salty,' he remarked. 'Very salty. In a good way. And chewy.' He noticed the grass verge between the pavement and the road and realised how hungry he was. 'I gotta feed the brain before I can think again,' he announced. And that was that. He started grazing.

He was right about needing food though, and the others joined him for a quick, brain-reviving snack. The grass was short and dusty but better than sand. They were wandering along, still nibbling at the verge, when Chas and Arnie arrived.

Both men had damp yellow sand sticking to their sweaty faces. Chas, looking hot and bad-tempered, emptied sand from the many pockets in his hoodie as he walked. Arnie was grinning from ear to ear. He gazed at the laminated certificate he was holding proudly in front of him.

'First prize . . .' he said, still surprised and delighted. 'Awarded to Arnold for the best sandcastle in the Over Twelves' Summer Class.' He waved the certificate in front of Chas's face. 'I've never ever had a first prize before. Not for anything.'

'Yours was the only one left standing,' grunted Chas unkindly. 'That's why you got it.' He unlocked the van and slumped into the driver's seat. 'I just don't understand,' he said for the umpteenth time. 'It was a classic swap. Calm. Professional. The egg, the money, the timing. And then . . . *sheep*.'

Arnie was still gazing at his certificate.

'I think it was the lolly sticks that won it for me.'

'Will you get your brain in gear!'

Chas snatched the certificate. Arnie snatched it back and stuck it in his pocket.

'How are we going to find the egg woman?' demanded Chas.

Arnie didn't answer. He was staring at the end of the street. The end that led from the beach. A woman wearing a sundress, a white linen jacket, an orange baseball cap and enormous sunglasses had just appeared and was walking towards them. She was cradling a plastic carrier bag in her arms.

Chas followed his brother's gaze. 'Hang on . . .' he breathed. 'That's the other one. The one with the cash. Get in the van.'

'What about me bike?' said Arnie.

'Never mind your stupid bike,' spluttered Chas. 'Sling it in the back. Get in quick. Don't let her see you.'

Arnie did as he was told and jumped in beside Chas.

'What's the panic? She doesn't know us. She's only

85

seen us once before. And we were being buried alive by a socking great sheep.'

'Sshhh . . .' Chas ducked his head down until the woman had walked past. 'Quick. Follow her!'

'Eh . . .?'

Chas made a turning motion with his arm. 'Do a three-point turn, bonebrain.'

'How am I supposed to do that?' Arnie demanded. '*You're* in the driving seat.'

Chas paused for a moment, then, with a sniff, turned the key in the ignition. He turned the van around and drove slowly along the road, keeping just behind Sunglass Woman. The rear doors, which Arnie hadn't had time to close properly, swung gently to and fro.

The little flock of Rare Breed sheep had grazed almost to the other end of the street when the woman with the carrier bag walked past them. With their noses still in the grass, they didn't see her and she was too busy dabbing at her mobile phone to see them. Then the van drove slowly past, its rear doors still swinging.

Wills raised his face from the grass.

'That van was in the pub car park,' he said. 'I'm sure it was.'

'So?' mumbled Oxo.

'So, maybe we should hitch a lift,' said Links. There was a sudden note of urgency in his voice.

'Why would we want to do that, dear?' asked Sal.

'Because that lot's comin' straight for us. And they look well annoyed.'

The sheep all looked up. Marching towards them from the direction of the beach was a crowd of people, led by the sandcastle judges.

'There they are!' shouted one of the judges. 'Round them up before they cause any more trouble!'

The crowd started to run.

'Round *yourself* up!' shouted Oxo and he launched himself at the van.

He timed his leap between the swinging doors perfectly and crashed on to the floor of the van, sending cans and bottles rolling this way and that. Then he leant against one of the doors to hold it open while the others leapt and scrambled in. The others except for Wills. He'd just helped Sal with a shove from behind when the van suddenly increased speed, leaving him standing alone in the middle of the road. Chas had put his foot down on the accelerator.

Sunglass Woman was no longer walking along the street. She'd unlocked a car, thrown her carrier bag full of cash on to the back seat and got in. The car was old, dented and splashed with mud but expensive-looking. And fast. Now it was racing out of town with the Thickett brothers in pursuit.

'I bet she's fixed somewhere else to swap her cash for the egg,' shouted Chas above the roar of the van's engine and banging of its rear doors. 'She'll lead us straight to it. Sure as eggs is, er . . . eggs.'

Behind the van, Wills was losing ground.

'Run, Willsyboy, run, man!' called Links desperately.

Then the van screeched to a sudden halt. Wills gathered his last remaining strength. He raced up and sprang inside.

The others were already squashed in beside Arnie's bike, toolboxes, lengths of wood, metal pipe, tins of paint and big plastic bottles marked with a black cross. Some of the bottles that had fallen over had lost their lids. Their contents were seeping out across the floor. Wills crouched down next to Links, panting for breath.

They all kept low as they heard footsteps running from the front of the van.

Wills just had time to read the label on one of the fallen bottles before the swinging doors were slammed shut and everything went black. The footsteps ran back to the front of the van, another door slammed and the journey resumed. Faster than ever. Wills sat in the dark, trembling. The label on the fallen bottle had read:

TOXIC. DO NOT INHALE.

7

Enigmata

'What's that smell, dears?' asked Sal, wrinkling her nose.

'Ohmygrass . . .' Jaycey began to cough. 'I don't know but it's making me feel weird. In the head.'

'Nothing new there then,' Oxo joked. But he too was beginning to feel rather sick.

'My eyes is streamin', man,' said Links. 'This is one bad vibe.'

'I think,' spluttered Wills, 'we should try to get out. We're being poisoned.'

None of the others knew what 'poisoned' meant but they all knew they were feeling worse by the minute.

'Can you . . .' Sal wheezed loudly, 'can you . . . help us, Oxo, dear?'

There wasn't enough room for a run-up so Oxo just

lowered his head and bashed it against the doors. The van rocked violently, the doors creaked but the lock held fast. Oxo sank to his knees, then rolled over on to his side. He felt very sick.

For the next fifteen minutes there was silence inside the van. Wills had no idea where they were going and, although he didn't say so, he doubted they would be alive when they got there.

Chas and Arnie had felt the van rocking when Oxo thumped the doors but assumed it was caused by toolboxes falling about inside. And they were too intent on following the woman with the carrier bag full of cash to care.

Sunglass Woman finally stopped in the village of Godshill. It was a pretty place, its one street lined with tea gardens and gift shops. Chas followed her as she drove into the big car park, pulling up nearby. Arnie baled out immediately.

'Where's that smell comin' from?' he asked. 'It's 'orrible.'

'We're in the country, Arnie. It often smells. Get over it.'

Chas stayed where he was in the van, gazing around. 'Look at all those coaches . . . And all the people. Good place for a swap.'

'Yeah,' said Arnie sarcastically. 'Just like the beach was.'

'Difference is,' said Chas, 'no sheep. Now stop moaning about the smell and get ready to follow her the moment she moves.'

But the woman with the bag of cash didn't move. She sat in her car, took her mobile phone from her jacket pocket and keyed in a number.

'Candy . . .?' she said when her call was answered. 'Is that you?' She spoke in a hushed voice, even though nobody could possibly hear. 'Where are you now?'

'On the bus,' said Candy. 'Like you told me. I'm heading for . . .'

'Shhhh! Don't say it.' Sunglass Woman adjusted her sunglasses and glanced left and right over her shoulders. 'Buses have ears.'

There was a moment's silence. Then Candy spoke again. She sounded irritated.

'So how am I supposed to answer your question?'

'Don't answer it. Just give me an ETA.'

'ETA?'

'Expected time of arrival.'

'Oh. Right.' There was a pause while Candy looked at her watch. 'I'll be you-know-where carrying you-know-what in about five minutes.'

'Good. Now listen carefully. The bus will stop right outside Ye Olde Village Tea Garden. Walk right across the garden. On the far side you will see a gateway to the model village. I will be sitting at a table close to that gateway.'

'How will I know you?'

'I will be wearing the same dark glasses, white jacket and orange cap. Order a pot of tea and a cream scone. With strawberry jam.'

'I don't like strawberry jam.'

'Don't argue . . . Put your bag, *the* bag, on the floor by your feet.'

'Right. Then what?'

'I will put *my* bag on the floor by *my* feet. We will have our tea. We will look nonchalant. When we've finished, I will leave first, taking *your* bag with me. I will exit via the model village. You will give me two minutes, then you will pick up *my* bag, walk back across the garden and exit into the main street. Is that clear?'

'Crystal clear.'

'Good. Over and out.'

'Hang on, hang on.' Candy's voice was agitated. 'What if it all goes wrong again? How do I get in touch with you? What's your name?'

Sunglass Woman opened then shut her mouth. A beam of sunlight glinted on the bracelet she was wearing, picking out the letters engraved on it: RUTH. She noticed and crossly shook the bracelet up inside her sleeve. Careless of her. If buses had ears, car parks may have eyes.

'You don't need to know my name,' she whispered into her phone. 'But you can call me . . .' she paused. 'Enigmata.'

'Call you *what*?'

'Enigmata. And this operation will also be given a code name. You will refer to it as Operation Ovum.'

'Right,' said Candy with a deep sigh. 'Anything you say. Let's just get on with it, shall we?'

'Exactly. And if you do as I say nothing will go wrong.'

'Unless a bunch of random sheep appear out of nowhere and muck everything up again.'

'Lightning doesn't strike twice. Random sheep certainly won't.'

Enigmata finished the call, popped the phone into her pocket and adjusted her huge sunglasses. She had a moment's doubt about the sunglasses: maybe they were so big, they weren't a disguise at all. She dismissed the thought and stepped out into the car park, tucking the carrier bag full of cash under her arm.

'That's it! She's moving at last,' cried Chas. 'Go, go, go . . .!' He flung his door open and tried to hurl himself out. But was instantly jammed back into his seat. He'd forgotten to unbuckle his seat belt.

'What are you waiting for, Arnie?' he shouted angrily as he struggled to undo the belt clasp. 'After her!'

Arnie forgot the unpleasant smell and hurried after the woman with the plastic carrier bag. Trying not to laugh.

The sudden jolting, as Chas struggled with his seat belt, revived the semi-conscious sheep lying in the back.

'We've stopped,' croaked Wills. 'Oxo, we've got to get out. Try one more time. Please!'

'Got to get out . . .' gasped Jaycey.

'Get out . . . got to get out . . .' baaed the others.

Bang! Oxo's great head whacked the van doors. They creaked but didn't open. The others shifted aside to give him a bit of room. He backed away, his eyes streaming, his nose and throat raw. Then he rumbled forward for what he knew would be the last time. His woozy brain was no longer talking to his legs.

Crash! Oxo hit the doors so hard even his bony forehead hurt. Daylight briefly blinded him. He seemed to be running in the air. Then he landed heavily at the feet of a large knot of holidaymakers.

The holidaymakers were elderly and anxious. They'd just got off a coach marked GOLDEN OLDIES ADVENTURE TOURS, but instead of heading straight for the tea garden, they'd been drawn to the van by the banging and pitiful baas they could hear. Now they gasped as they saw yet more sheep stumbling out of the van.

A pretty little Jacob landed behind the big ram. She was shaking and whimpering and coughing. Then a slightly smaller ram, with woolly ringlets, half-jumped, half-rolled out. His eyes were red and streaming and he too was coughing. Finally, a large ewe emerged from the semi-darkness. She stood trembling in the open doorway.

In her mouth she was holding a limp and entirely motionless lamb.

8
The Model Village

'Ohmygrass . . . OhmyWills . . .' sobbed Jaycey, scrabbling to her hooves, and vainly trying to reach up to him and Sal.

Others got there first.

Sal suddenly felt human hands under her tummy and she was lifted out of the van and lowered carefully on to the ground. Once safe, she dropped Wills gently from her mouth, then began licking him as if he were her own newborn lamb.

It took a few anxious moments and a lot of licks from Sal's strong tongue before Wills' eyes opened. And a few more before he lurched to his feet.

'I'm OK now, Sal,' he said weakly. 'Really I am. Thank you . . .'

The crowd of humans were as relieved as Sal when they heard the lamb bleat. They oohed and aahed as he took a few wobbly steps. But once they were sure he was going to survive, their relief changed to indignation. What kind of person shuts animals in the back of a van full of chemicals? Chas had finally undone his seat belt and was climbing out of the van when the angry crowd turned on him.

'How could you be so cruel?' someone shouted. 'You shouldn't be allowed to keep animals.' The crowd pressed closer.

'You should be reported to the RSPCA,' called another voice.

'And the police,' called another. 'You're a disgrace!'

Finally Chas made his voice heard above the anger. 'Look, I've got no idea where those animals came from!' he shouted. 'No idea at all.'

'He's trying to pull the wool over our eyes,' shouted a voice from the back.

'Yeah. He must think we're daaaft,' shouted another.

Chas began shoving his way roughly through the hostile crowd. He was desperate not to lose sight of his brother.

Arnie was waiting just along the road, outside Ye Olde Village Tea Garden. He was anxiously eyeing the crowd still gathered near the van.

'Talk about not drawing attention . . .' he muttered, as Chas arrived.

'Whose fault is that?' snapped Chas. 'I nearly got torn limb from limb back there. And all because *you* didn't notice the van was chock full of sheep. Thanks a bunch.' He glared at Arnie. 'Where is she?'

'Other side of the lawn,' said Arnie. 'Sitting near the model village.'

Chas peered through the gateway, saw Sunglass Woman and nodded. 'And the other one? The one with the egg?'

Arnie shrugged. 'No sign of her yet.' A moment later his worried frown was replaced by a big grin. 'Forget that. Here she is.'

'Where?'

'Behiiiiind you . . .'

Chas turned. An open-top bus had just pulled up outside the tea garden: the Sunshine Special. First off, before the holidaymakers with their cameras and guide books, was a tall, slim, dark-haired young woman in a denim skirt, T-shirt and black lace-up boots. She had a pink duffel bag hooked firmly over her shoulder.

Arnie wasn't the only one to spot the new arrival. The Warriors, even Wills, had more or less recovered, and were edging away from their crowd of admirers when they saw the bus pull up.

'Look!' cried Jaycey. 'Looklooklook! Getting off the bus. It's her. The woman with the dragon's egg. Ohmygrass . . .!'

They all looked towards the bus.

'Jaycey's right, innit,' said Links. 'What we gonna do, guys?'

Sal drew herself up to her full, not very high, height. 'We are going to face our Moment of Destiny,' she cried. 'We are going to destroy the egg and save the world!'

'Yeah! One for five and five for the world,' shouted Oxo. 'Charge!'

And, led by the great Oxford ram, the Warriors galloped into Ye Olde Village Tea Garden.

Until that moment it had been a peaceful spot. The neatly mown lawn was dotted with elegant, spindly-legged chairs and equally elegant tables covered with white cloths. The lawn was edged with flower beds brimming with pink and purple blooms. A little fountain tinkled in the centre and a lady tinkled on a harp in one corner. Customers drank tea from china cups and discussed how to eat the gorgeous cakes without getting cream and jam all over their chins.

Oxo saw none of this. He was entirely focused on the young woman hurrying across the lawn with the dragon's egg in her pink bag. Unfortunately there were obstacles. And Oxo never went round obstacles. The first to get in his way was a waitress with teapots, sugar bowls and milk jugs balanced on a silver tray. The next was a waitress carefully holding, on one arm, a platter laden with cream cakes. Both waitresses went down. And both trays went up. There was a gasp of horror. Then the tea, sugar, milk and cakes rained down on customers at the nearby tables. The customers jumped to their feet, tipping chairs backwards and tables forwards. Sponge cakes, meringues and chocolate éclairs flipped from their plates and splatted on to clean shirts and skirts. More cake joined the tea, sugar and milk on the grass.

Oxo, followed by the other Warriors, charged on, skidding through the cream and jam and chocolate, ignoring the shouts and screams.

Candy had just sat down with Enigmata when the

commotion began behind her. She leapt up again and span round to see what was going on. She saw a ram, smeared with cream and chocolate, heading straight for her. It would have been funny but for the look in his yellow eyes. There was no doubt about it. They were fixed on her and her alone.

'You said there wouldn't be any random sheep this time!' she cried at Enigmata. Then, without waiting for a response, she clutched her pink duffel bag to her chest and ran through the exit into the model village.

'Not that way! That's my route,' Enigmata called after her. 'You're supposed to go out on to the road –'

Her words were lost in a crash of teacups and saucers as the Warrior Sheep barged their way past more tables and chairs and also disappeared into the model village.

Enigmata sat very still and straight. This should have been such an easy operation. Starfish had said it couldn't possibly fail. And Starfish didn't like being proved wrong. She wasn't looking forward to explaining that she had been thwarted twice. By a bunch of sheep.

Chas and Arnie were still standing on the pavement

outside the tea garden. They'd been too astonished to move when the sheep had charged past them. But as the woman with the pink bag hurried off into the model village, they finally got a grip on their wits.

'Ignore the crazy sheep,' barked Chas. 'Don't let her get away!' He raced on to the grass, promptly trod on a cream cake and skidded into one of the few tables still standing.

''Scuse us,' he called as he ran on, leaving a lady scraping lemon drizzle from her glasses.

The brothers skated through the tea garden, straight past Enigmata, who was still sitting rigidly at her table, and burst into the model village.

It was perfect, laid out neatly with pretty streets, a village green and a real stream. Most of the buildings were about knee-high, some had lights on inside and others had miniature people in their miniature gardens.

Candy was weaving along the little streets but the pursuing flock of sheep were agile and determined and gaining on her. At last she did an about-turn and instead of running around the model school, she leapt over it.

The big ram skidded round to follow her but he was

going too fast to jump. He ploughed straight through the school and the other sheep followed. Little tables, chairs and whiteboards crunched under their hooves. Candy glanced behind at the wreckage then hesitated, not sure which way to go next.

Chas saw his chance. Excitedly he plonked his feet on either side of the little road that led from the wrecked school building to the church. He bent his knees, spread his arms wide and waited for the woman with the pink duffel bag to run into them. He was so focused on the woman, he didn't see the great ram behind her.

'Arnie! Grab the bag!' he yelled.

But Arnie wasn't about to grab anything. He *had* seen the ram.

The woman with the pink bag veered sideways and took a giant leap over the model church. The ram didn't.

Oxo hit Chas like a woolly torpedo. The next moment Chas was in the church. At least his head was. His feet were in the demolished school. Little bells began to ring in the church tower, matching the loud and painful bells ringing in his head.

The Warriors didn't stop to look at the man Oxo had flattened. The woman with the dragon's egg in her pink bag was escaping from the model village on to the real street. The sheep were only a hoof-step behind when their luck ran out.

The bus that had brought Candy to Godshill was still there. One lot of passengers had got off and another lot had got on. The seats on the open top deck were now full of people leaning out to photograph the chaos in Ye Olde Village Tea Garden. The seats inside were full of people scraping cake from their clothes and hair.

The driver revved the engine and Candy leapt on board just before the door hissed shut. She turned and gazed through the glass at the five sheep still on the pavement. They gazed steadfastly back. And continued to stare as Candy was carried away.

'Well that's it, innit?' said Links. 'We lost her again.'

'I really can't run any more, dears,' said Sal. Her knees buckled and she sank on to the pavement.

Wills was thinking hard. 'Maybe you won't have to, Sal,' he said. 'The bus she got on was called the Sunshine Special. I read it on the side.'

The others waited expectantly.

'And?' asked Oxo, already being distracted by a tasty dollop of cream on his shoulder.

'And it said where it was going,' said Wills. 'It said it was going to somewhere called Alum Bay Only.'

'Well *done*, dear,' said Sal. 'So, er, how do we get to Alum Bay Only?'

Wills trotted over to the bus stop. 'On the next bus, hopefully,' he said. 'I'll find out how long we've got to wait.'

'Ohmygrass . . .' fussed Jaycey. 'Will they let me on looking like this?' She began nibbling grass and grit and strawberry jam from her fleece.

'I'll have the jam if you don't want it,' said Oxo, finishing the cream from his shoulder. 'Tasty stuff this tea garden.'

'Man, you is disgusting,' said Links.

Sal watched anxiously as Wills slowly worked out the numbers on the timetable. Finally he turned to face her.

'What's wrong, dear?' she asked.

'There's only one bus a day,' said Wills unhappily. 'And that was it.'

9
The Golden Oldies

Arnie had experienced a moment of indecision. Should he help his torpedoed brother or should he follow the woman with the black boots and pink bag? He'd looked at Chas lying spread-eagled across the model village and started to giggle. Laughing at Chas was never a good idea so he turned and ran back through the tea garden. He arrived on the pavement just as the bus pulled away. But, like Wills, he saw where it was going.

By the time Chas had picked himself up and limped back to the street, Arnie was driving the van out of the car park.

'Get in quick,' he ordered.

Chas hauled himself painfully into the passenger seat.

'What happened to the nuclear sheep?' he asked.

'They're not in the back again, are they?'

'Nah. I checked. Doors are busted but I tied them shut.' Arnie grunted. 'Mr Fixall's not gonna be best pleased when he gets his van back.'

Chas picked a clump of greasy white fleece from his hoodie. He rolled it between his fingers then flung it out of the window.

'I could have been lying there dead,' he said. 'Did you care?'

'Not a lot,' said Arnie, and he started to giggle again. 'Ding-dong, ding-dong.'

'Very funny.' Chas turned and glared out of the window at a group of elderly people on the pavement. One of the ladies noticed the van and shook her stick at it. Chas looked away quickly, glad he couldn't hear what she was saying.

'That's the lot from the coach we parked next to,' he said. 'Golden Oldies Adventure Tours.'

'Oh, right,' said Arnie. 'The mob that nearly tore you limb from limb?' But then he stopped smirking. In his wing mirror, he could see an elderly gentleman from the group photographing the back of the van – and possibly its number plate – using his mobile phone.

'Uh, oh . . . What sort of prison sentence d'you get for cruelty to sheep?' he asked.

'Will you shut up about sheep?' Chas picked chocolate cake from his hair. 'Where are we going, anyway?'

'Thought you'd never ask,' said Arnie smugly. 'We're following the Sunshine Special. All the way to Alum Bay!'

Only a few of the elderly people on the pavement were interested in the departing van. The rest were listening to their coach driver.

'I'm afraid Ye Olde Village Tea Garden is going to be closed for the rest of the day,' he was saying. 'They've got a health and safety issue with cake on the lawn. But I've booked you into a very nice place not far away. So if you'll all get back on the coach, please . . .'

Some of his Golden Oldie passengers began to drift back to the car park and for the first time the driver saw the little flock of five sheep on the pavement behind them. His mouth dropped open.

'What about these?' asked the old lady who had

waved her stick at the departing van.

'Well, they're not coming with *us*,' declared the driver.

'But those brutes in the white van might come back for them,' said the lady with the stick. 'We can't leave them here.'

'You're quite right, Violet . . .'

'Out of the question . . .'

'Absolutely not . . .'

'Well said, dear . . .'

The chorus of voices agreeing with Violet grew louder. Violet grew bolder.

'Of course,' she said, 'I think I speak for us all when I say we have been very happy with you as our driver, Dave. And we *were* planning to club together to give you a nice tip at the end of our holiday.'

'The others nodded meaningfully. 'We *were* . . .' they chorused.

Dave hesitated. His Golden Oldie passengers were smiling politely but their eyes all had a glint of steel. School kids were so much easier.

'*Surely* we could just take them to safety?' said Violet. 'Where did you say we're going?'

'I didn't. But we're going to Alum Bay.' Dave made up his mind. 'And we're *not* taking sheep.'

The Warriors had remained quite still from the moment the elderly humans had surrounded them. They could tell that some of them weren't very strong, and didn't want to knock them over. The flow of human voices had rippled across their heads but now two words jolted Wills into action.

'Alum Bay,' he whispered excitedly. 'They're going to Alum Bay! Maybe they'll give us a lift. Come on, guys. Try to look appealing.'

'Peeling what?' Oxo looked round for apples he could get his teeth into.

'Not peeling. *A*ppealing!' Wills struggled to explain. 'Cute and . . . and pretty and . . .'

Links snorted with laughter. 'Guess that leaves you out, man,' he said to Oxo.

But Jaycey's turn to shine had come. She raised herself on tip-hoof and did a little shimmy. Then she gave the closest pair of human legs a playful little butt. The legs happened to belong to Dave.

He couldn't help himself. He looked down at

112

Jaycey and smiled.

'Ahhh . . .' said Violet. 'See. She likes you.'

'She likes you,' chorused the Golden Oldies.

'Way to go, Jaycey,' giggled Wills. 'High hooves!' He raised and clacked a front hoof with Jaycey. Then he scampered off towards the coach and the rest of the Warriors and all the humans followed.

'They're not to sit on the seats!' ordered Dave as his passengers clambered aboard.

The sheep had no intention of sitting on the seats. They were perfectly comfortable lying in the aisle. They couldn't see where they were going but that didn't matter. They knew they were heading for somewhere called Alum Bay which hopefully was the same as Alum Bay Only. And that they weren't far behind the girl with the dragon's egg.

They were back on the road and Links began to nod.

'We is the Warrior Sheep
An' we is back on track.
We ate a lotta sand
An' we took a lotta flak,
But the travellin' Golden Oldies

113

Is our golden oldie friends.
They got us on the road again
No matter where it ends.
We is focused on our mission
An' for us there ain't no match.
We's gonna nail the dragon,
That egg will never hatch.'

The humans had no idea what all the noise was about
but they all clapped and tapped their sticks as the rest
of the Warriors joined in the chorus.

'We is focused on our mission
An' for us there ain't no match.
We's gonna nail the dragon.
That egg will never hatch!'

Candy hadn't intended to go to Alum Bay. She didn't
like the place at all. All she had wanted to do when
she jumped on the Sunshine Special was escape from
the crazy bunch of sheep. Especially the big ram with
the yellow eyes. But she needed time to think so she
found an empty seat inside and sank into it. She was

sweating and thirsty and confused. What had seemed like a simple way to make a lot of money had become very un-simple. Who *was* Enigmata, anyway? Why did she want the dinosaur egg? And what did she know about the sheep? It was the sheep that really worried Candy. She was no nearer answering any of her own questions when her phone rang.

'Enigmata here,' the voice said. 'What went wrong with plan B? Over.'

'Wrong?' squeaked Candy. 'Random sheep! That's what went wrong.'

'I suspect dirty tricks,' said Enigmata. 'Our phones are probably being hacked, even as we speak.'

Candy took her phone from her ear and looked at it. How could sheep hack into a phone? And how would she know if they had? She shrugged and held it to her ear again. Enigmata was still speaking.

'Where are you now? Over.'

'In la-la land. Like you,' replied Candy.

'There's no need to be rude.'

'Well, if I tell you *where* I am and someone *has* miraculously hacked the phones, they'll know too.'

'I see the problem.' There was a long pause. 'But

it's a risk we have to take. Go ahead, please. Over.'

Candy sighed. 'I'm on the Sunshine Special heading for Alum Bay. And I'm sweaty, thirsty and hungry.'

'Too much detail. Are you listening? Over.'

'*Yes.*'

'When you get off the bus, sit on the wall by the flower beds and await further instructions. Do you copy me?'

'Eh?'

'Understand?'

'Yes.'

'Good. Over and out.'

Back on the Golden Oldies' coach, Wills was singing along with the other Warriors. He was also thinking about Tod and Ida. None of the humans sitting in the coach looked *quite* as old as Ida but some of them were getting close. Wills hoped his own special humans were enjoying whatever it was they'd come to the Isle of Wight to do.

In fact, Tod and Ida *were* having a wonderful time. In less than a day, the trailer in Rex Headland's shed had

116

been transformed. It no longer looked like any old farm trailer. The carpenters had built a huge platform, which they'd secured to the base, and the painters were busy painting this green. At the same time, the electricians were rigging up light bulbs to flash on and off in sync with the music and the sound engineers were installing the speakers. Tod was helping bend wire into fantastic shapes ready for the sewing team to cover in fabric and sequins. And Ida was dashing around, instructing, advising and generally getting stuck in. Loving every second. She and Tod turned as Fred Jolliff arrived with a bale of straw that Ida has asked for.

'How are our sheep doing?' Tod asked, bending a wire into a loop bigger than himself.

'Oh, I bain't been out to Penny Pasture yet today, nipper, but I'm sure they be fine.' Fred laughed. 'You be acting like a mother hen. But I'll go over there shortly if it puts yer mind at rest.'

'That's very nice of you,' said Ida. 'I know we do fuss a bit but they have managed to get themselves into all sorts of trouble in the past.'

'They'd have a job here,' said Fred. 'Nothing much ever happens on the Isle o' Wight.'

10
Egg Over the Cliff

'Alum Bay,' announced Dave the driver. 'Sheep off first, please.'

The Golden Oldies called goodbye as the Warriors scampered out of the coach.

'They do seem to have a mind of their own, don't they?' remarked Violet. 'But I still think we should report those Mr Fixall men to the police.'

'Done, dear lady,' said the elderly man who had photographed the van's registration number. He waggled his mobile phone at her. 'Handy little things these. Wish we'd had them when I was a youngster.' He winked at Violet. 'I could have texted you and asked for a date.'

'Tea and cake this way . . .' shouted Dave over the hubbub of cars and coaches, buses and people. Alum Bay was a busy holiday park. 'Follow me, please.'

The Golden Oldies hurried after him. What could be better than sunshine, a coach driver who allowed sheep on-board, and tea and cake.

Having set off at a run, the Warriors had now slowed to a halt. They peered through the crowds that milled around the many ice cream parlours, cafes, amusement arcades and sweet shops.

'Don't see a pink bag anywhere,' grunted Oxo.

In fact the pink bag and its owner were in a cafe, queuing to buy a veggie burger. Candy was still queuing when Oxo decided he needed to eat too. He led the other Warriors to a patch of grass and shrubbery away from the crowds and they got their noses down.

'Man, it tastes like fish and petrol,' complained Links.

'What's not to like?' mumbled Oxo.

They grazed in silence for a short while before Sal eventually lifted her head. Something had caught her eye way up in the sky. 'Am I imagining it, dears,' she said, 'or are those humans flying?'

The humans she was looking up at were sitting side by side on metal benches high above her head.

'I shouldn't think they're flying . . .' said Wills with a giggle. He looked around then nodded at a tall metal tower nearby. 'See that tall thing?' he said. 'I think it's called a pylon . . .'

'A pie *what*?' asked Oxo. 'Doesn't look much like a pie to me.'

'Not a pie. A py*lon*,' said Wills. 'There are three of them: that one, another one closer to the cliff and one right on the cliff edge. And can you see the cable stretched between them?' The others nodded. 'Well . . .' Wills was getting excited. 'The benches those humans are sitting on are attached to that cable by long rods. Can you see?' The others nodded again. They could. 'And the cable's moving along between the pylons, which means the rods are moving along too,' he finished triumphantly. 'Taking the benches with them.'

'How interesting, dear,' said Sal, though she didn't have a clue what Wills was talking about.

Wills trotted to the cliff edge and peered over. It was a long, long way down to the beach. More pylons, holding the moving cable aloft, jutted at a crazy angle from the cliff. Wills realised that the cable formed a never-ending loop, going from the top of the cliff down to the beach at the bottom and up again. It just went on and on, without a pause, taking the benches with it: down and up, down and up . . .

Wills watched, delighted and envious, as the benches passed over the cliff edge. The humans, with their legs dangling in mid-air, clutched each other and squealed and shrieked as they swayed slowly down to the beach.

Looking around again, Wills saw a wooden hut and a little platform where the cable loop started. He trotted across and watched what happened. People paid their money, and then stood on the platform, waiting for the next bench. As soon as it was beside them, they jumped on, two to a chair. A metal bar clanged over their laps and they were carried slowly towards the cliff edge and then . . . they were out of sight.

Wills was so excited, he forgot about the dragon's egg and the Warriors' mission. 'Come and see this, guys,' he called. 'It's brilliant! It's called a chairlift,' he said, nodding in the direction of the sign hanging from the hut.

The others joined him.

'It's so clever,' exclaimed Wills. 'See, it goes round and round in a loop and humans can jump on or off at either the top or the bottom. There's a platform just like this one on the beach. It never stops.' He sighed. 'I wish I could have a go.'

'Why?' asked Oxo. 'Is there grub down at the bottom?'

'Ohmygrass . . . Ohmyno*thanks* . . .' said Jaycey. 'You'll never get *me* on one of those.'

Jaycey wasn't the only one not keen on the Alum Bay chairlift. Candy hated it. Not that she was thinking about it right now. She was still queuing for a burger. When she finally got to the front of the queue she bought a double-decker and smothered it in ketchup, then sat on the wall by the flower beds, just as Enigmata had told her.

Chas and Arnie were wandering towards the same wall. Chas was too nervous to eat but Arnie had gone one bigger than Candy. He was trying to get his mouth round a burger as big as his head.

'Eat quietly,' said Chas crossly.

'When did Dad ever say that?' asked Arnie. 'I don't remember him being particular about table manners.' He slurped up a long trail of greasy fried onion.

Chas suddenly froze.

'Ditch that!' he ordered. 'She's here. They're both here!'

Arnie looked up and saw Sunglass Woman striding towards the flower beds with her carrier bag full of cash. He saw Candy too. He looked down at his burger, looked sideways at Chas, then stuffed the whole treble-decker into his mouth.

'Wo way am I witching it,' he mumbled.

Neither of the women saw Chas and Arnie. Sunglass Woman perched on the wall beside Candy.

'Good afternoon. I am Enigmata.'

'Yes, I know.'

'You don't have a code name. An omission on my part. I will call you Raven.'

'I'm quite happy with Candy –'

'Ssshh! OK, Raven. Operation Ovum. Take three. Have you got the you-know-what?'

Candy – or Raven – sighed and patted the pink bag on her lap.

Enigmata nodded. 'And I have the other you-know-what.' She patted her carrier bag.

Candy held out her pink bag. 'Swap?' she said.

'Not here,' snapped Enigmata. 'Too public. Follow me.'

'Oh, for goodness' sake!'

But Enigmata was already on her feet. She strode towards the chairlift.

'Not the chairlift . . .' Candy gasped in horror as she realised where Enigmata was going. 'I hate the chairlift. It makes me sick.'

'Nonsense.' Enigmata fumbled in her pocket, got out her purse and bought two tickets. 'That's all in the mind.' She strode over and stood behind the small queue of people waiting for a chair.

Candy hurried over and stood beside her. She was feeling trembly. 'It's not in the mind. It's in my stomach. Then all over my feet.'

A few steps behind them, Chas was trembling too, but with excitement.

'This is perfect,' he said. 'Right, Arnie . . . Any minute now . . . We grab the bag just before they get on the chairlift. Right?'

'Which wag?' Arnie managed to ask through his mouthful of burger.

'The pink one, bonebrain.'

'Bit public, isn't it?' asked Arnie, swallowing the entire bottom deck of bun and beef. 'What happened to not drawing attention to ourselves?'

'We won't draw attention to ourselves. We'll be like greased lightning. Gone before anyone knows what's happened. And the beauty of it is, *they'll* be stuck on the chairlift heading for the beach with just a bag of cash between them.'

'Can't we just nick the cash? It'd be a lot easier.'

Chas shook his head in despair. 'You have no aspirations,' he said.

Arnie had never realised that. He wasn't sure if it was a good thing or not.

A couple of holidaymakers in front of Candy and Enigmata hopped on to the next empty chair. The attendant clamped the safety bar across their laps and they swung away, up towards the cliff edge.

'Our turn next,' said Enigmata. 'Are you ready?'

Candy drew a deep breath. 'I'm ready,' she said. 'What can *possibly* go wrong?'

Enigmata missed the sarcasm. 'Nothing. But just in case it does, we will no longer communicate by leaky technology.' She took a piece of paper from her pocket and held it out to Candy. 'This is a list of further rendezvous points. In order. Read. Remember. Destroy.'

Enigmata's handwriting was bold and clear and Candy read the information in one glance.

'OK, I've remembered it,' she said.

'But you might forget again,' said Enigmata. 'Take it!'

Candy raised her eyebrows. She was holding her pink bag in one hand and her untouched burger in the other. She didn't have a spare hand to take the list. Enigmata slid it into the burger, under the lettuce and tomato garnish.

The next empty chair had appeared over the cliff and was approaching the platform.

'*Come on*, Raven!' ordered Enigmata, as she slid into the slowly moving seat.

'*Grab and run!*' ordered Chas and he dashed at Candy before she had time to move. He snatched the bag from her shoulder, then shoved her on to the seat beside Enigmata.

'*Charge!*' roared Oxo.

A flock of galloping sheep arrived on the platform,

scattering attendants and holidaymakers in all directions.

'My bag, my bag!' cried Candy.

But her chair was already moving away. She and Enigmata both twisted round in their seat. They watched, open-mouthed, as the heavy ram who'd been charging towards Candy, pivoted on four hooves and smashed into the man who'd stolen her bag. The animal's head acted like a bulldozer and shoved the thief on to the next chair coming round. Unable to stop, the ram skidded on after him and scrabbled on to the seat.

Candy and Enigmata faced forward again. Their chair was swaying above the treetops now and Candy was beginning to feel nauseous.

Back on the platform, Links was determined to be part of the action. He waited until the next chair was alongside, then ran towards it. Unfortunately, the man in lime green lycra got in his way. Arnie stumbled head first on to the chair and Links barged on after him. The chair swayed alarmingly as Links scrabbled to get on to the seat,

'Woah, sit still, man,' the Lincoln Longwool said.

'Or we is beach pizza.' Then he yelled excitedly at the chair in front. 'Nice one, Oxo! I'm right behind you, dude.'

As Oxo, Links and the pink bag swung out of sight, Wills turned to Jaycey and Sal.

'We have to get down the cliff. There must be a path. Come on!'

Wills dodged away through the legs of the nearest attendant. The man barely noticed. He was too busy arguing with his colleagues. Should they halt the chairlift or not? Invasion by sheep wasn't mentioned in the safety regulations.

There *was* a path, a steep one with steps, more or less under the flight path of the chairlift.

Wills bounded down towards the distant beach, trying not to envy Oxo and Links their spectacular ride.

Jaycey skipped nimbly behind and Sal wobbled and bounced at the rear.

'Your boldest deeds you now must match,' she puffed. 'This dragon's egg must *never* hatch!'

Then she missed her footing and rolled the rest of the way like a woolly boulder.

Oxo was feeling pleased with himself. That change of direction, from charging at the *woman* with the bag to the *man* with the bag, had been pretty nifty, he thought. But he wasn't sure what to do now. He was sitting with his rump on the seat and his front hooves over the bar. Not a good position from which to butt. He edged his bottom a bit closer. The man hugging the bag gave a little yelp of fright and budged over. Oxo grinned and moved closer still. Soon the man was so squashed he had to turn sideways on the seat. Oxo twisted his neck and tried to grab the bag between his teeth. The man yelped louder. He held the bag aloft with one hand and tried to beat the sheep off with the other. But Oxo knew he was winning and wasn't going to give up.

In the chair in front, Candy tried to forget about feeling sick. She forced herself to twist round in her seat to see what was happening. She saw the dangling bag and the sheep's large snapping jaws. The teeth, she noticed with shivering dread, were as yellow as the sheep's eyes. She turned forward again, her head and stomach swimming.

The chair behind her was swaying violently now as

Oxo lunged again and again. Terrified that the animal was going to bite him, Chas suddenly lowered his aching arm. He banged his elbow on the safety bar, yelled with pain . . . and dropped the pink bag.

11
Read, Remember, Destroy

The chair Candy and Enigmata were sitting on had just reached the beach platform when Chas dropped the precious pink bag.

Candy was ready for it. She'd seen enough of the tussle to realise what was bound to happen. She forgot about feeling sick. Leaping out on to the platform, Candy dropped her burger and hurled herself headlong on to the beach. She caught the bag, one-handed, inches from the ground.

As Candy scrambled to her feet again, Enigmata was already riding helplessly away back up the cliff. She hadn't seen the pink bag fall. She'd been astonished when Candy dived out after it and had been much too slow to follow. Her bench had moved onwards and up and all she could do was shout orders.

'The list!' cried Enigmata. 'Get the list. Read . . .

Remember . . . Destroy . . .' Her voice was lost in the whirr of chairlift machinery. And the bleats of the large ram behind her as it launched itself into space.

Oxo landed badly. He rolled over and over and got sand in his eyes and up his nose. Candy stood staring at him in horror. Then two voices cut through all the other noise. Both of them male.

'Arnie! Why are you just *sitting* there?' Chas had twisted round in his seat and was shouting at his brother in the chair behind. 'Get after the egg! I'll follow the money.'

'Great!' Arnie shouted back. 'Why do I always get the best jobs?'

'Because you're the youngest. Jump!'

Arnie ducked under the safety bar and jumped. The ram with floppy curls had already baled out of the seat beside him.

'Still with you, Oxo man!' called Links, as he jumped.

Candy stared aghast at the shower of men and sheep raining down. She took a step back towards the chairlift, then saw that the ram with yellow eyes was struggling to his feet. She didn't dare try to pass him. She backed slowly away, desperately wondering what to do. From the corner of her eye she saw the burger lying on the sand. She bent sideways and scooped it up, never taking her eyes off the big, grunting sheep. She wasn't interested in Enigmata's ketchup-smeared list, which was still stuck under the lettuce garnish. She remembered every silly word of it. But maybe the burger would be useful. The ram suddenly pawed the sand, lowered his head and charged straight at her. Candy screamed. She threw the burger as hard as she could at the ram's head. Then she turned and ran the other way.

The burger hit Oxo between the eyes then plopped harmlessly on to the sand. Oxo snaffled it up – waste not, want not – then he galloped after the woman with the dragon's egg with Links hot on his hooves.

'We're coming too!' cried Wills from the bottom of the steps. And he and Sal and Jaycey joined the chase.

Candy was fast and nimble. As she neared the headland at the end of the beach, the sand and shingle gave way to rocks, slippery with seaweed, and soon she was splashing through the waves. The tide was coming in.

She glanced over her shoulder and was relieved to

see that the sheep were losing ground, their hooves slipping and sliding on the boulders. The man in green lycra, running behind them, was also slowing. A wave slapped hard against his side. He staggered and sank to his knees as the tide whooshed out again. Then another wave surged in, soaking him up to his armpits this time. Candy watched as he lurched to his feet and started trudging back towards the chairlift. She turned and ran on.

Once round the headland, Candy began to climb the cliff. It was difficult but not steep here: more a massive tumbledown heap of gorse and grass and stunted trees. Soon she was out of sight.

Far behind, the sheep stumbled to a gasping halt.

'I think, dears,' wheezed Sal, 'it's time to regroup . . .' And she collapsed in a regrouping sort of way.

'Respect, though, man,' said Links to Oxo. 'Runnin' all that way with your mouth bunged up.'

'Mmm?' mumbled Oxo. He opened his mouth and the soggy burger dropped out. 'Oh. Forgot all about that.' He peered down at it. 'Lettuce looks a bit limp now but it might be all right.' He snaffled the burger up again and started chewing.

'Stop!' Wills had seen the piece of paper sticking out of the bun and was suddenly excited. 'Stop, Oxo. Don't eat the paper!'

'What paper?'

Oxo dropped the burger again and Wills used his front hoof to slide the paper out of the bun. He stared hard at the ketchup-smeared words, then read them slowly aloud.

FOR RAVEN'S EYES ONLY
THIS IS A LIST OF RENDEZVOUS FOR YOU-KNOW-WHAT.
(TO BE FOLLOWED IN THE EVENT OF UNFORESEEN
PROBLEMS.)
1. SANDY BAY BEACH. (FAILED)
2. YE OLDE VILLAGE TEA GARDEN. (FAILED)
3. CHAIRLIFT AT ALUM BAY.
4. FOOTPATH AT PENNY PASTURE.
5. BLACKGANG CHINE.
DON'T FORGET: READ, REMEMBER, DESTROY.
ENIGMATA

The Warriors stood in silence for a moment once Wills had finished reading.

'Erm . . . is that useful, dear?' asked Sal.

'Very,' said Wills. 'I think. I don't know what rendezvous means but we know now where the woman with our dragon's egg is going next. All we've got to do is get to Penny Pasture before she does.'

Sal nodded. 'I see.' Wills could tell that she didn't see at all.

'We saw her at Sandy Bay,' he explained, 'then at the tea gardens, then on the chairlift. I don't know *why* she's taking the egg round to all these places, but I'm pretty sure she'll be at Penny Pasture next. You remember Penny Pasture? The field where we started?'

Sal nodded. 'Of course, dear.' This time she did understand. 'And if we don't get it from her at Penny Pasture, we follow her to the *next* place on the list.'

'Exactly,' cried Wills.

'So why do we have to destroy the list?' asked Jaycey.

Wills shrugged. 'I don't know. But it'll be easier than trying to carry it.'

'I could keep it in my mouth,' offered Oxo. 'There's plenty of room.'

'Nah, we should remember it, innit,' said Links. 'Like it says.'

'*I'll* remember Penny Pasture,' said Sal.

'And I'll remember it too,' promised Jaycey, not wanting to be left out.

'I'll do Blackgang Chine,' said Links. 'Cool name.'

'All right then,' said Oxo. 'I'll do the destroying.' He snarfed up the paper again and started to chew. It wasn't bad with ketchup on.

'Well *done*, dears,' said Sal.

A wave suddenly rolled in and covered their hooves. Then another.

'We should get off the beach,' said Wills. 'Or we'll have to swim.'

'What, in the *sea*?' demanded Jaycey. 'That's worse than sheep dip. Ohmypoorfleece!'

Looking up at the tumbledown cliff, they glimpsed the woman with the pink bag at the very top.

'Onwards and upwards!' cried Sal.

And onwards and upwards they went.

When Candy got back to Alum Bay, she called a taxi to take her home. The sun was going down. It would be dark in a couple of hours. She was still hungry, and also dirty, tired and cross. Enigmata had told her *where* to meet next but not *when*. What good was that?

Enigmata realised her mistake when she was in her car several miles from Alum Bay. She'd vowed not to phone Candy again in case their phones were being hacked, but there was no choice.

'Ten a.m. tomorrow. Over and out,' was all she said when Candy answered.

Enigmata had slipped away from all the fuss and bother at the top of the chairlift without being noticed. And before the guy with the cake-smeared hoodie had been able to follow. She drove home wondering how she was going to explain that once again she'd failed to get the dinosaur egg. Starfish would be kind as always. Understanding. But disappointed. Starfish expected things to go smoothly. For Starfish, failure was not an option.

Arnie trudged wearily up the steps to the top of the cliff. Chas was waiting for him. Anxiously. The police had arrived and were glancing in his direction as they talked to the chairlift attendants.

'Well . . .? Did you get it?'

'Course I didn't get it,' snapped Arnie. 'I'm a human being, not a mountain goat.'

Chas stumped away to the van. 'We're finished,' he groaned. 'Done for. There's no way we're going to get the egg now.' He threw himself into the driver's seat. 'We don't know where the woman with the egg's gone. And we don't know where the woman with the cash has gone.'

Arnie slumped into the passenger seat. 'You were on the chairlift behind her,' he moaned. 'Why didn't you follow her when you got to the top?'

'Because she's got a super-fast car and we've only got this stinky old van.' Chas heaved a big sigh. 'We might as well go home.' He sighed again, then realised that Arnie was grinning. 'What's so funny?'

Arnie continued to grin. Then he announced, '*I* know where we can find her. The one with the cash.'

Chas stared. 'How?'

Arnie held out his hands, both fists tightly closed. 'Right or left?'

'Right . . .' said Chas.

Arnie opened his right hand. It was empty.

Chas turned away angrily. 'Arnie, I'm not in the mood for silly games!'

'Don't you want to know what's in the other hand?' Arnie teased.

Chas sighed. 'All right . . . all right . . . Left.'

Arnie slowly opened his left hand. Lying flat in his palm was a small pocket diary. 'Take it,' he said. 'Look who it belongs to.'

Chas took the little diary and opened it. His eyes widened. His jaw dropped.

'Where d'you get this?' he asked.

'I didn't nick it,' said Arnie. 'I rescued it.'

Chas nodded but he was barely listening now. He was flicking through the pocket diary.

Arnie beamed with pride. 'When she took out her purse to buy the tickets, this came with it. She didn't notice. You didn't notice. But *I* did.'

Chas flopped back in his seat, suddenly all smiles. He was staring at the front page of the diary. Written in neat, bold handwriting were the words: *This diary belongs to Ruth Pemberton-Smith, Wisteria Cottage, Old Mill Street, Ventnor.*

12
The Bale of Straw

Ruth lived in a small cottage in the town of Ventnor. Chas and Arnie spent a very uncomfortable night in their van taking turns at staying awake to watch the front door. Nothing happened until they both fell asleep at the same time, just before ten o'clock next morning. Ruth (code name Enigmata) came out. She glanced at the white van parked just up the road, wondered briefly where she'd seen it before, then forgot it and set off for Penny Pasture.

Ruth felt rested and confident. Penny Pasture was just a brisk walk away. The footpath behind it was quiet and secluded. She patted her strong new carrier bag full of cash. Nothing could go wrong this time. Really.

The Warriors had woken much earlier. They'd spent a comfortable night under a nice big gorse bush at the top of the cliff, but they were now eager to be on their way. Wills said they should find a signpost pointing towards Ventnor. He knew Tod and Ida were staying in Ventnor and guessed Penny Pasture wasn't far from there. The downland grass under-hoof was soft and springy and they had gone quite a few miles before the sun came up. But still no signpost.

Wills was getting worried. 'I think we've still got a long way to go. If you remember how far we came in that stinky van and then the coach.'

The others shuddered at the memory of the van.

They trotted on for a good few minutes before Wills suddenly cried, 'Bus stop!' He set off down the hill at top speed. The other Warriors peered at the road below, then scampered eagerly after the lamb.

'I think we need the Island Breezer,' said Wills, trying to understand the timetable. 'That goes to Ventnor. If we haven't missed it.'

The driver of the Island Breezer was bored. He hadn't yet picked up any tourists. They were still tucking into their 'full English' breakfasts.

Then, up ahead, he saw customers at the next stop.

He blinked and slowed the bus to a halt.

'Where do you lot think you're going?' he asked, looking down at the little flock of sheep standing in line on the grass verge.

'Baaaaa . . . baaaa . . . baaaa . . .'

The driver opened the doors for a closer look. The sheep sprang aboard and trotted straight up the stairs. The driver didn't think he could haul them off by himself so he shrugged and drove on.

'D'you want sheep day returns?' he called, but nobody answered.

It was a beautiful morning and a beautiful ride. The Warriors stood on the top deck of the open top bus with their front hooves on the rail, enjoying the breeze rippling their fleeces. The sea sparkled on their right and soft green hills rolled gently upwards on their left.

Wills didn't really want the ride to end but after about half an hour he suddenly recognised the road they were now humming along. They'd come this way from the ferry.

'Quick, we're almost there. Penny Pasture's just round the next bend.'

The Warriors scrambled down the stairs and

stood expectantly by the doors.

'You're supposed to ring the bell if you want me to stop,' said the driver. But he braked and opened the doors for them. 'I called Island Radio and told 'em I had a bunch of sheep on the top deck. They said, "*Ewe* must be joking." So I said, "No. It was just a *shear* coincidence." And they said . . .'

But his passengers had jumped off the bus now, so the driver closed the doors and drove away, waving at the sheep left standing by the roadside.

The Warriors turned on to a narrow footpath. Soon they were standing beside the signpost to The Dragon's Nest and the hole Oxo had made in the hedge.

'Not bad, eh?' said the big Oxford, admiring his headwork.

'No sense, no feeling,' sniffed Jaycey.

'Mind if I wriggle through for a quick snack?' Oxo didn't wait for an answer. He squeezed his way back into the field.

The others followed.

'But we must stay just here,' said Wills, popping through last. 'So we hear when the woman with the dragon's egg comes along the path.'

They had only just begun cropping the sweet grass when the gate at the far side of the field opened and three people came in.

'Sal . . . Oxo . . . Jaycey . . .'

The sheep from Eppingham Farm looked up.

'Ohymgrass!' cried Jaycey. 'It's Tod and Ida.' She galloped down the slope to meet them.

'Links . . . Wills . . .' called Tod.

All the other sheep galloped after Jaycey and came face-to-face with Tod, Ida and Fred Jolliff in the middle of the field.

'See . . . I told you they be safe and sound,' said Fred, raising his eyebrows at Tod and Ida, who were patting and fussing over their sheep. 'They bain't hardly moved.'

'I know . . . it was silly of us to worry,' said Ida. 'And it's really very good of you to bring us out to see them.'

Fred laughed. 'Well, I was gonna take a photograph to show 'ee but the woman in the chemist's says they don't develop black and white film no more. It's all digital or summat, these days.'

Ida straightened up. 'We mustn't take any more of your time,' she said and started walking back to the gate.

Tod gently scratched the top of Wills' head. 'And there we were thinking you might have gone galloping off across the Island.' He jigged up and down excitedly. 'I wish you could see what we're making, Wills. It's truly awesome. Best float Gran's ever designed. And just wait till we get the dancers trained up.'

The sheep followed Tod and Ida to the gate and everyone stood in a cosy little group waiting for Fred Jolliff.

Fred was at the top of the field, peering at a large hole in the hedge.

'That weren't there afore,' he muttered, kicking aside broken twigs and leaves. He glanced at his own large flock, suddenly worried that some might have escaped. They were too many to count accurately right now but all seemed to be there, dotted about the field. Fred turned back to the hole and spoke to it.

'I can't stop to repair 'ee now but I'll have to plug 'ee with summat.'

His eye was caught by an old bale of straw he'd left inside the lambing shelter in the near corner of the field. He hauled it out and dragged it across to the hole.

'Get in there, darn 'ee . . .' he grunted, shoving the bale into the hole. He stood back to inspect it. 'Bain't a pretty job but it'll keep they sheep in.' He wiped his hands on his trousers and grunted. 'Keep an elephant in, that will.'

He hurried away to join Tod and Ida by the gate. They'd been too engrossed in their Rare Breed reunion to notice what Fred had been doing.

The Warriors were still enjoying being petted when Links spotted the woman with the pink bag pedalling along the road.

'It's her, innit?' he said urgently. 'Dragon's egg woman!'

Jaycey stuck her head through the bars of the gate. 'She's getting off the bike thing. She's on hoof now. Ohmygrass . . . I can't see her any more.'

'She must have turned on to the footpath,' said Wills. 'Quick!'

With Oxo in the lead, the Warriors suddenly charged away towards the top of the field.

Tod laughed. 'Never know what's in their minds, do you, Gran?'

Fred, Tod and Ida were climbing into Fred's old

truck, ready to head back to Ventnor, when the sheep reached the far hedge.

'Bye!' called Tod and Ida as they drove away. But the Warriors didn't notice. They'd just discovered that there was no longer a nice big hole in the hedge.

'Ohmygrass!' cried Jaycey. 'We're trappedtrapped-trapped!'

'I can hear the woman breathing, innit!' said Links. 'The dragon's egg's right *there*. On the other side of this . . .' He butted the straw bale but it didn't move.

Wills was listening to something else. A new set of soft footsteps on the path.

'Oxo, let me stand on your back for a sec,' he whispered.

From his wobbly viewpoint on Oxo's back, Wills could just peep over the hedge. He could see the woman with the pink bag stomping impatiently up and down. And he could see Sunglass Woman hurrying along the footpath towards her. Wills didn't understand why these two women kept meeting. He was sure it had something to do with the egg and he feared that Sunglass Woman wanted it for herself. And if she got it, who knew where she might take it?

'You've only got one chance, Oxo,' he breathed urgently, leaping down from the great ram's back. 'It's now or never. Go for it!'

Oxo lowered his head, then lifted it again, squinting.

'What's wrong?' whispered Jaycey.

'Just takin' aim, innit,' Links reassured her.

Oxo squinted harder, lowered his head again, pawed the ground with his front hoof and rolled his shoulders.

'Charge!'

Candy and Enigmata were in smiling distance, almost touching distance when the footpath seemed to explode. A straw bale suddenly blasted between them. It burst its binding tape and straw shot and showered in all directions. The long, scratchy, yellowish stalks stabbed their skin like knitting needles, and the short, dusty bits got into their eyes and throats, making them cough.

'Aarrghh . . .' wailed Candy. 'Now what?'

She shook straw violently from her face. And saw the huge ram with yellow eyes standing between herself and Enigmata. Candy picked up her pink bag and fled. Never mind her bike. She would run round the world backwards rather than pass that ram to get to it.

Enigmata stood for a moment, gazing after the rapidly disappearing Candy. Then she peered at the ram. It hadn't moved since its dramatic appearance. She was suddenly intrigued. Was it *real*? Or was it . . . some sort of *spy* device? She strode over and poked it, hard.

'Baaa . . .'

Oxo's head swung round and Enigmata took a quick step backwards. It was real enough. But why was it there? She peered over the hedge into the field. The other four sheep were trying to scramble through the hole after the ram.

It had become obvious to Enigmata. Somebody *must* be controlling them. She scanned the field but saw no one. Controlling them remotely then. That must be it. But why? Did someone else want the egg? If so, who? And why were they using the sheep to get at it? Operation Ovum was in jeopardy.

Enigmata marched away, spitting out straw. She needed to speak to Starfish about the sheep.

She needed permission to eliminate them.

13
The Truth About Ruth

Oxo stood very still on the straw-covered footpath.
Too dazed to move or even blink. The other
Warriors clustered around him.

'Ohmygrassohmyoxo! He's not *dead*, is he, Sal?'

'I don't think so, Jaycey.' Sal peered into Oxo's eyes.
'Have you hurt your head, dear?'

Oxo didn't move.

'HAVE YOU HURT YOUR HEAD?'

Nothing.

'Ask him if he wants this big cabbage,' said Wills.

'Cabbage? Where?' Oxo turned his head sharply
towards Wills, then rolled it from side to side. He
shook it vigorously and blinked several times.

'Just testing,' said Wills. 'But the next big one we
come across is all yours.'

'That was your best hedge bust ever, innit,' said

Links. 'We is proud of you, man.'

Everyone agreed.

'But we *still* haven't got the dragon's egg,' said Jaycey. 'And if we don't destroy it soon, the baby dragons will hatch and spread fire and famine and bad breath across the whole entire world for ever and ever. That's right, isn't it, Wills?'

'Uh. Yes.'

'Ohmygrass!'

'Don't worry, Jaycey,' said Wills. 'If we go to the next place on the list we found, we'll find the woman with the pink bag again.' He looked round. 'Who remembered the next name on the list?'

Nobody spoke. Then Links gave an embarrassed little cough.

'Er . . . I think that was down to me.'

'Oh, purleeze . . .' Jaycey tossed her head and turned away. 'He's only *forgotten*.'

'Don't hassle me, man.' Links glared at Jaycey but only because he was suddenly feeling very guilty. 'It'll come.'

The others watched as he walked round in a circle muttering, 'Black. I is sure that the first word is black.

But what the second is . . .? Black*foot* . . . black*tongue*
. . . black*hoof* . . .? Nah, they is all like nasty diseases.
Black*bottom* . . . black*gate* . . .? Nah, not gate . . . ga,
ga, GANG! Blackgang!'

'Phew!' Wills raised his front hoof. 'High hooves!'

Links raised a front hoof and clacked it against
Wills'. 'High hooves. Sorry 'bout that, guys.'

'So where is this *Blackgang*?' demanded Jaycey.

'I think I saw some signs when we were on the
bus,' Wills replied. 'If we go back along the road a bit,
I'm sure we'll find one that tells us which way to go.'

'First cabbage is mine, remember,' said Oxo as they
all trooped off.

Wills was right. The Isle of Wight was full of
footpaths and signposts and the sheep were soon
trotting along the coastal path, with Blackgang Chine
only two miles away.

'Are we going fast enough, dear?' said Sal. 'We
don't want to miss her.'

'I think we're fine,' said Wills. He couldn't help a
giggle. 'She looked really scared at Penny Pasture. I
expect she's regrouping like you do, Sal.'

*

153

Candy was indeed regrouping: at home, with the curtains closed. She'd always thought of herself as a strong person but the sheep were really getting to her. As soon as she felt well enough, she checked her email. There was one from her boss at the museum, Mr Adams, asking how she was getting on with her egg investigations. She replied:

No luck yet. How are the police doing?

The response was instant.

> **They're not even trying. Too busy hunting down this flock of rogue sheep causing havoc everywhere.**

Candy promised to keep trying, then sat back, feeling a little happier. Maybe the sheep, especially that ram, weren't targeting just her, after all. She was still pondering when her phone rang.

'Enigmata here. Thirteen hundred hours. Fairyland. Over and . . .'

'No!' Candy screeched into the phone. 'Over and

154

back. Or it's *all* over.'

There was a pause.

'This is very irregular, Raven.'

'Will you stop this stupid spy stuff?' snapped Candy. 'I don't care if the phones are tapped. I want answers. One. How did you know about the egg?'

Another pause, brief this time. 'We read about it on the website, of course.'

'*We?* Who's *we*?'

'That really doesn't concern you.'

'OK. But twenty people work at the museum. Why pick on *me* to do your dirty work. What made you think I'd be interested?'

The answer was clear and concise. 'Because you're bored, Candy. With your job, your friends, the Island, everything. You want excitement, you want to travel, have fun. But you haven't got any money. You were ripe for crime.'

Candy's jaw dropped. She swallowed hard. 'How do you know all that?'

'I heard you tell your hairdresser. Apart from the ripe for crime bit.' Candy's mouth opened again but this time no words came out. Enigmata continued.

'And as you accepted my offer, you *are* now a criminal. I'll see you at you-know-where. Over and out.'

Candy chewed her lip for a while, then ran down into Ventnor. The hairdressing salon was busy but one of the stylists, Lisa, had a few moments to spare. She flicked back through the appointment book.

'Why do you want to know?' she asked.

Candy had her lie ready. 'It's not for me, it's for my brother. He's seen her around and really fancies her.'

She felt herself blush. Enigmata was right. She *was* a criminal. And now a liar too.

Lisa glanced up and smiled. 'Ah, sweet.' She found the page.

'Right. When you were last in, I was doing Nell's cut and blow-dry . . .?'

Candy shook her head. She knew Nell.

'Kim was doing Mrs Sharp's roots.' Lisa grinned. 'Mrs Sharp's nearly seventy so I don't suppose it was her your brother fancied. And Paul was looking after Ruth Pemberton-Smith . . .'

'What's she like?'

'About thirty. Small, slim, elegant. Blonde bob. A bit odd but very nice.'

Candy clenched her teeth. Small, slim, elegant, a bit odd. That would be the one. She thanked Lisa and hurried home. She found the name Ruth Pemberton-Smith in the phone directory and called the landline number. A woman answered. Candy recognised the voice.

'Hi, Enigmata . . .' She left a long pause. ' . . . Or can I call you Ruth?'

It was Enigmata's turn to be shocked.

'How did you get . . .?'

'That really doesn't concern you.' Candy rather enjoyed repeating Enigmata's own words. 'But we're on a level playing field now. *You* could shop me to the police and *I* could shop *you*. So where do we go from here?'

There was another pause, then Enigmata said, 'We meet you-know-where, you-know-when.'

'What if those sheep turn up again?'

'I'll be ready for them.' Enigmata lowered her voice. 'I think they're being controlled.'

'*Controlled?*'

'By the guys in that white van.'

'That's the stupidest thing you've said yet.'

Enigmata's response was deadpan. 'The only other explanation is that the sheep want the egg for themselves. And how ridiculous is *that*?' She paused. 'We meet again as planned. And if the Mr Fixalls or their sheep attempt to stop us, they'll be sorry. Over and out.'

Chas and Arnie woke up with a start. They were unaware that Ruth had been out of the house and come back home again, spitting straw. Now, a late breakfast seemed a good idea. Chas sent Arnie to fetch it.

Arnie came back with two jam doughnuts and a local newspaper. He looked disappointed.

'Thought I might be on the front page,' he said.

'What for?'

'Me sandcastle.'

Chas groaned.

'But it's all about those sheep.' Arnie quoted from the paper, '"*A flock of rogue sheep have been rampaging around the island leaving a trail of destruction.*"'

'Tell me about it,' grunted Chas, sniffing the congealed cream, which was beginning to smell distinctly unpleasant on his shoulder.

Arnie read on in silence, then looked up thoughtfully. 'Did Dad have anything to say about sheep?'

Chas shrugged.

'Not that I know of.'

'Just as well probably,' said Arnie. 'You're always quoting his words of wisdom but answer me this: if he's such a master criminal, how come he's spent most of our lives behind bars?'

Chas's mouth was too full of doughnut to give an answer. He didn't have one anyway.

A moment later, Arnie spoke again. Quietly. He was staring up the street. 'Chas . . .'

'Mm?'

'Her car's gone!'

Over in the huge shed at Headland Manor, Ida was also reading the local newspaper.

'Well,' she said with relief, looking up at Tod, 'at least it can't be *our* sheep this time. They're behaving themselves in Penny Pasture.'

'Right, Gran,' said Tod, taking the newspaper from her. 'We've seen them with our own eyes. Now, let's concentrate, shall we?'

With only one day to go, carnival activity in Rex Headland's shed had reached fever pitch. The float was almost complete: the lights worked, the sound effects worked and the music worked. The last glittery gauze had been sewn on to the costumes and pots of face paint and body paint were stacked ready for use. An excited, chattering group of people who would be dressed in costumes and walking alongside the float were waiting to hear their instructions.

Tod stood on a chair and called for silence.

'Gran's just about lost her voice with all the talking she's been doing,' he said, 'so I hope you won't mind if I speak for her.'

'Carry on, young man,' called Rex. 'You have our full attention.'

'Right.' Tod grinned. 'Most of the time you'll be just walking, obviously, but every time the float stops you'll be doing a little routine.'

There was a gasp and ripple of panic from all those who never danced.

'Don't worry. It's very simple. Gran'll demonstrate. I'll call the moves.'

Ida turned her back to the group so they could follow her movements.

'Ready?' called Tod. 'After four. Step forward on the right foot. Tiny lift of left foot. Step backwards on the right foot, tiny lift of left foot. OK?'

It was, even for those who'd always thought they had two left feet. Tod carried on.

'Do that three times.'

Everyone did.

'Now turn to face the crowd. Look fierce. Take two ordinary steps forward, then flap your arms twice.'

There was a lot of giggling as people tried to flap and look fierce.

Tod grinned and shouted the next instruction.

'Turn and walk two steps back. Shake your tail twice.'

Even more giggling. Tod had to shout the last line even louder.

'Now turn slowly to face the front. Take four beats. Good. And now you're ready to start again.'

Some of the dancers ended up facing the front, some ended up facing the back and some were laughing so much they didn't move at all.

'Shall we walk through that once more?' called Tod. 'And then we'll try it to the music.'

The dancers were walking through the routine again, with slightly better results, when a young woman with neat, blonde hair popped her head round the door.

Rex Headland, who was standing at the back of the shed, beaming and tapping his feet, saw her and waved. He made his way to the door. Outside in the yard, he gave her a big hug.

'Hello, Ruth. How's my favourite niece today?'

Ruth (code name Enigmata) smiled and gave Rex a peck on the cheek.

'Fine, thank you, Uncle Rex. But we need to talk.'

14
Fairyland

The Warriors stood on the coastal path, looking down at Blackgang Chine's huge car park and the sea beyond. Wills read the big sign at the entrance:

WELCOME TO OUR FANTASTIC THEME PARK

'What's one of them?' asked Oxo.

'I don't know,' said Wills, 'but it sounds like fun.'

They found a spot under the trees, from where they could see everyone going in and out of the car park, and settled down to wait. Gales of laughter and the squeals of excited children wafted up to them.

It wasn't long before a battered car swept into the car park and a familiar pair of huge sunglasses got out. Sunglass Woman strode to the entrance, paid her money, and walked in past the gigantic model smuggler that guarded Blackgang Chine.

'Her again?' said Wills. He wasn't surprised. But he was worried. 'I'm sure she wants the egg too. But what for?'

'Dunno,' said Oxo. 'But the other lot are here an' all.'

They all watched as the white van, with its back doors tied together with rope, drew up. The two men they'd seen before jumped out and hurried past the giant smuggler.

'Yeah,' agreed Links. 'It's them again, innit. Man, that dragon's egg is hot property.'

'Not too hot, I hope.' Sal shuddered. She'd misunderstood Links. 'If it gets *too* hot it'll start to hatch.'

When Chas and Arnie realised they'd missed seeing Ruth leave home, they'd spent some time blaming each other. Then they'd taken turns to nip along to some public toilets to get washed. Chas had done his best to scrub the cream and jam from his hoodie but it still smelt a bit ripe. They were both back in their van when, to their relief, Ruth returned. She dashed indoors, and came out again a few moments later, clutching her carrier bag. She dived back into her car and this time Chas was ready.

But so was Ruth. She immediately spotted the Mr Fixall van in her wing mirror. She watched it follow her the short distance from her home to Blackgang Chine, then draw up and park nearby. Whoever these guys were, they weren't exactly the best undercover agents in the world. Ruth made a brief phone call.

'Starfish? Enigmata here. I'm definitely being followed. Men in van. No sheep yet but suspect they may be deployed at any moment. Your assistance required. ASAP.'

Up in their shady spot under the trees, the Warriors continued to watch and wait for the woman with the pink bag. They were just beginning to worry that they might have missed her, or that she wasn't coming after all, when Jaycey suddenly stiffened.

'Ohmygrass . . . I can smell dog. Whereisitwhereisit?'

A large truck had drawn up in the car park. A tall, slim, upright man stepped out. He wound the window right down and spoke to the dog inside.

'Don't like the look of that,' muttered Oxo. 'It's a Border Collie.'

'Yes, but I don't think we need panic, dears,' said Sal. 'It won't be interested in us.'

She'd hardly finished speaking when Links cried out. 'This is her, innit!'

He had spotted the young woman with dark hair, denim skirt and black lace-up boots, cycling down the slip road to the car park. The bulging pink bag was strapped across her chest.

Candy liked Blackgang Chine; had done since she was a little girl. It was a theme park with something for everyone: a fairyland for little ones, a pirate ship for older children to climb on, a cowboy town, a rollercoaster ride, a maze, a hall of funny mirrors. She still enjoyed going there but she couldn't understand why Enigmata had chosen it as a rendezvous. It was always so busy. Perhaps that was the point. The quiet of the path behind Penny Pasture hadn't worked. So maybe it *was* safest for criminals to meet in a crowd. Candy shivered at the word 'criminal'. Was she really a criminal now?

The Warriors watched her dismount.

'Onwards and downwards?' asked Oxo.

Without waiting for an answer, he plunged downhill through the scrubby trees that clung to the cliff above Blackgang. The others jumped and slithered after him. They galloped across the car park, past the giant smuggler's legs and slid to a stop at the ticket desk in the large entrance hall.

'One adult, please,' Candy was saying to the man behind the till.

'What about them?' asked the man. 'You can't take sheep in.'

Candy turned, saw the sheep and screamed. The nightmare was beginning again. She didn't wait for her ticket. She barged through the barrier and burst out into the sunshine beyond. The Warriors raced after her.

Wills had been right about Blackgang Chine. Theme parks were obviously fun. A trail wound away down the cliffs and a big signpost explained what exciting things the crowds of visitors would find on every level.

Pink Bag Woman was shoving past parents with buggies and eager children and heading for the first stop on the trail: Fairyland. Wills and the rest of the Warriors followed.

In Fairyland, Ruth (code name Enigmata), was waiting calmly beside the Magic Pool. Gnomes with fishing rods bobbed up and down all around her. Enigmata was rather pleased with the location. It was crowded with families but they were all distracted by fishing gnomes, fairy fountains and talking flowers. Nobody would notice two women swapping bags. Uncle Rex had also approved, which was good.

Chas and Arnie lurked out of sight beneath a giant spotted toadstool. Ruth knew they were there but she wasn't worried because Uncle Rex was also close by.

Rex Headland himself was standing, feeling slightly foolish, behind an enchanted tree and trying not to jump every time it shouted, 'Ho, ho, ho.'

Ruth looked up sharply. The sound of families having fun had suddenly changed to cries of alarm.

Then Candy burst into Fairyland, shoving aside everyone in her path. Ruth waved, and held up the bag full of money, but if Candy saw, she wasn't interested. She glanced round desperately. A ram with yellow eyes appeared behind her and she ran blindly on.

For a moment, Oxo was thrown by the huge purple plastic flower that suddenly leaned over and said 'hello' to him. But Pink Bag Woman had raced past it and so did he. She dropped to her knees and frantically crawled into the child-sized entrance to the Enchanted Castle. Oxo tried to follow but his body was much too wide. The tower shook and children on the balcony above laughed as he backed out again.

Candy crawled right through the Enchanted Castle and out the other side. She struggled to her feet beside the Magic Pool. But the ram had spotted her again. She gave a little cry and leapt over the Magic Pool in one bound. Even Oxo's legs weren't long enough to jump the pool so he plunged in and waded through it. The other Warriors followed.

'Ohmygrass . . .' cried Jaycey, distracted as a magic fountain suddenly showered her with glittery, pink water. 'Ohmyglitter. This is *such* a good look.'

As Candy landed, Ruth stood up and grabbed her arm. 'Raven, stop!'

But Candy shook her off violently and Ruth fell backwards into the pool. A second later, she was knocked under by a tidal wave of sheep. Gasping, she picked up a bobbing gnome that had fallen in with her and hurled it after the sheep.

Rex didn't try to stop Candy as she hurtled past his enchanted tree. These sheep had to be dealt with first. As the great soggy ram galloped by, Rex leapt out and grabbed the scruff of his neck. Bracing his feet, he hauled a surprised Oxo backwards to a halt. Then swung a leg across his back and sat there like a cowboy on a horse.

Oxo bucked and reared, twisted and turned, but Rex held on tight.

'Keep still, you stupid brute!' he ordered, whacking Oxo's side with his hand.

'That is well out of order, man!' cried Links. He lowered his head and butted Oxo hard up the bottom. Oxo jolted forward. Rex lost his grip, shot over the ram's head and landed heavily in a patch of nodding, laughing plastic flowers.

'Nice one, mate,' called Oxo, turning to look for the woman with the pink bag.

'Any time, bro,' replied Links.

Candy was some way ahead now, heading for the sign marked EXIT. She raced on, followed by five wet sheep, Ruth, Rex, Chas and Arnie.

'Raven!' Candy had almost reached the exit hall

when she heard Enigmata's voice. It was loud and commanding. 'Raven! Stop! That is an order. Over and out.'

Candy looked round desperately then dodged sideways out of sight.

Oxo put the brakes on violently. 'Where'd she go?' he asked, looking round.

Then he almost jumped out of his fleece. He was suddenly standing face-to-face with a big ram. An Oxford, like himself. But with very short legs and an enormous head.

'Woah . . . where d'you spring from?' he asked.

The ram facing him opened and shut his mouth. He seemed to be mimicking Oxo.

'You being funny?' demanded Oxo. He glared angrily at the newcomer. The ram opposite glared back.

'Well you're standing right in my way, matey.' Oxo snorted. The ram opposite snorted too. 'And if you don't move, I'm gonna have to butt you out of it.' Oxo pawed the ground with his front hoof. The ram facing him pawed the ground too.

'That's it!' snorted Oxo. He put his head down. The ram in front of him did the same.

'Oxo! Don't!'

Wills' shout came a second too late. Oxo's head hit glass. Violently.

'Don't! It's a mirror!' Wills yelled again.

'What's one of them?' Oxo turned, a bit dizzy and bewildered. The ram with the short legs and enormous head had disappeared in a shower of broken glass.

'A reflection,' said Wills. 'Like in the duck pond at home.'

'Oh,' said Oxo. 'Didn't feel like a duck pond.'

Links, Sal and Jaycey had arrived in the Hall of Funny Mirrors now and were staring astonished at their own reflections.

'Ohmygrass . . .' cried Jaycey. 'I've gone cabbage-shaped!'

'An' look at my legs,' said Links. 'They is longest of long, innit.'

Sal was rather pleased with the reflection staring back from her mirror. She looked extremely slim, except for her face, which was oddly wavy. But this was no time for being amused.

'Did anyone see where she went?' she asked sharply. 'We *are* on a mission.'

The four humans, Rex, Ruth, Chas and Arnie, had also arrived. They ignored the mirrors. And for a moment, the sheep.

'There she is!' cried Ruth.

Candy dodged from behind one of the curved glass mirrors and barged her way through the watching crowd towards the exit. She was almost there when she tripped over a buggy and crashed headlong to the floor. She lay perfectly still, curled on her side, the egg, in its pink bag, clutched to her chest.

Oxo reached her first. He put his head down and tried to tug the pink bag from her shoulder. But a foot shoved him away. One of the staff was trying to restore order.

'Get this woman outside for some air,' she shouted. 'Call the first-aider. And the police!'

A group of volunteers gently picked Candy up and carried her towards the car park. Chas and Arnie tried to follow but the tall, silver-haired man shoved them aside.

'Don't panic, anyone. Everything's under control!' Rex Headland's strong, military voice cut through the hubbub. He was standing in the doorway now. He put his fingers to his lips and let out a piercing whistle. Within seconds, Queenie, his Border Collie, was at his side.

'Round 'em up, girl,' Rex commanded.

The Warriors found themselves in the worst possible situation a sheep could imagine: trapped inside a building with a dog.

Queenie growled in their faces, snapped and yelped and ran round and round until they were huddled together in a tight, terrified little bunch.

'Good girl,' called Rex. He turned to the Blackgang Chine staff and addressed them confidently.

'Carry on, chaps. And chapesses. I'll look after these little blighters till someone claims them.' And off he marched, with Ruth, her damp skirt flapping around her legs, trying to keep up.

After the volunteers had carried Candy outside, a kindly first-aider had arrived and sat Candy down on a chair near the exit. He was examining a bump on her forehead when Ruth, Rex and Queenie emerged with the flock of terrified sheep. Ruth glanced at the pink bag on Candy's lap. For a moment she was tempted to snatch it. But the first-aider suddenly took a blanket from his bag and draped it around Candy's shoulders. He tucked it in around his patient and the pink bag disappeared beneath it. Ruth sighed and hurried on towards the car park. She would contact Raven later and arrange another rendezvous. One the sheep or their controllers couldn't spoil.

'There's nothing to worry about,' the first-aider was saying to Candy as the Warriors were driven past. 'It was a nasty fall but you'll be OK. Now where do you live?'

'Ventnor,' said Candy, shrinking away from the sheep. 'Twenty-one Sea Street.'

Queenie herded the sheep away from the building, running this way and that to prevent any of them breaking away. She growled and bared her teeth, keeping her captive flock together as they trotted fearfully across the car park towards Rex's truck.

'Hold 'em!' Rex called sternly as he fished in his pocket for his keys.

Queenie lay on her belly, staring at the huddled sheep, daring them to move. Rex opened the rear doors of the truck and flipped down a metal ramp.

'Drive 'em in, Queenie. Good dog . . .'

Queenie nipped at Oxo's heels and he skittered up the ramp into the truck. The others hurried in after him. Rex quickly stowed the ramp and slammed the doors shut. 'Good *girl* . . .'

Inside the truck, Jaycey had buried her head under some straw but her body was still trembling. The others stood in subdued silence as the engine roared into life and they were carried away.

'Sorry, guys,' Oxo said eventually. 'Bit stupid there. Should've whacked the dog too. Butted her from here to Eppingham.'

'Don't be silly, dear,' said Sal. 'No sheep, even one as brave as you, can master a dog.' She glanced at a little sore bit on her ankle where Queenie had nipped her. 'And *she* was particularly doggish.'

They didn't speak for the rest of the short journey.

Eventually, the truck turned into the yard at Headland Manor. It passed the main shed where Tod and Ida and the carnival volunteers were gathered, admiring their handiwork, practising their steps and chattering excitedly. Unaware of the new arrivals.

The truck continued across two fields and finally

stopped outside a large airy barn.

Rex and Queenie herded the sheep from the truck into the barn.

'Will they be safe in there, Uncle?' asked Ruth anxiously, as she got out of her car.

'Safer than a prison,' said Rex. And he pulled the heavy barn door shut and slammed down the iron locking bar.

15
Trapped in the Barn

The Warriors huddled together in the dim barn, listening to the truck drive away.

'Ohymgrass . . .' sobbed Jaycey. 'Has it gone? Has that horrible bitey thing gone?'

'Hush, dear,' soothed Sal. 'It's gone. You're quite safe now.'

'It didn't get our Oxo did it? Or Links? Or Wills? Are we all here?'

'We're all here, innit,' said Links. He trotted to the door and nudged it with his nose. 'An' we might be stayin' here a while.'

'Oh, yeah?' Oxo charged the door hard, but rebounded. Dizziness returned. 'Hmmm,' he said. 'Yeah . . .'

The barn was large, clean and comfortable, with hay bales scattered about. Light filtered in through a window above their heads.

'I think that's our only hope,' said Wills, staring up at the window.

Links looked up. 'I'm not getting the *hope* vibes, man.'

Wills trotted over and stood beside one of the hay bales.

'You might if you help me move this. If we can get it over to the window, one of us can climb on it and see what's outside.'

'Respect,' said Links, and he set to work.

They took it in turns to stand, two at a time, behind the hay bale, shoving it with their heads, while the other three called directions.

'Left a bit . . . right a bit . . . stop!'

When they'd got it into position, Wills sprang from the floor on to the bale.

But it wasn't high enough. He still couldn't see out of the window. So the Warriors spent the rest of the afternoon nosing and butting hay bales around to form a set of steps they could all climb up. Links got them rapping as they worked:

'We is the Warrior Sheep,

We ain't bothered by no jail.

Takes more than doors to stop us

Cos we don't never fail.

We got brains as well as brawn,

To get us out of harm.

An' a dragon's egg needs smashin',

So it's "See yuh!" to this barn!

Yeah, the dragon's egg needs smashin',

So it's "See yuh!" to this barn!'

Wills bounded up the hay staircase and peered out of the window. There was no glass, just a curtain of cobwebs. The others waited expectantly to hear what he could see.

'It'll be easy enough to get down,' he said, 'but the dog's still there.'

Everyone groaned and fell into gloomy silence. Except Oxo.

'Oh, well,' he said. 'Missed lunch, didn't we? Might as well get stuck in.'

He began to devour the nearest non-staircase hay bale.

Everyone else joined in. It had been hungry work.

After a while they heard the distant noise of engines starting, car doors slamming and humans calling goodnight to each other.

Wills hopped up the hay bale steps and peeked out of the window. All was now quiet in the distant yard. And there was no sign of the dog.

Wills pricked his ears up and listened hard. He sniffed the air. Nothing. He looked back down at the others.

'I think we're clear,' he said, 'but I'm going out to check.'

He didn't give anyone a chance to object. Even though there would be no way back for him. He leapt down to the field outside and trotted cautiously away.

The others waited anxiously. It seemed a long time before they heard Wills' voice outside.

'All clear. You can come out now. One by one, though. Oxo first.'

Oxo leapt from the window and landed with a heavy thud some way away. Sal came next. She just rolled from the sill and splurged on to the grass. Links couldn't resist making a drama of it.

'Flyin' high, man!' he shouted as he launched himself from the window sill.

That left Jaycey. 'Ohmygrassitssofardown!' She teetered on the edge for a few moments then squealed and landed elegantly next to Wills.

'High hooves?' asked the lamb, who was bouncing with excitement.

'High hooves!' they all agreed, raising their front hooves and clacking them together.

There was a long pause after that.

'Um, it's fleecetastic that we're out of there . . .' said Jaycey. 'But what do we do next? I mean, we *sooooo* don't know where the egg's gone.'

'We *sooooo* do,' giggled Wills.

The others stared at him. He stared back, teasingly.

'Where?' demanded Jaycey.

'Twenty-one Sea Street. Ventnor!' Wills couldn't help sounding pleased with himself for once. 'I heard the woman with the pink bag tell the first-aid person.'

'Well *done*, dear,' said Sal.

'Yeah, tin-ribs.' Oxo gave Wills a playful nudge that knocked him off his feet. 'So where's Sea Street, then?'

Wills didn't know exactly but Ventnor couldn't be that big a place.

Excited by the new challenge, the Warriors galloped across the field, out of the manor gate, and headed into town.

Candy was still lying curled up on the couch with her thumb in her mouth when the Warrior Sheep eventually found Sea Street. She was wishing she'd never heard of the dinosaur egg. Wishing she'd never heard of Ruth, code name Enig-rotten-mata. And most of all wishing she'd never set eyes on the bunch of sheep who seemed out to get her. Would she ever be safe from that ram with yellow eyes? She closed her own eyes and waited for darkness. Maybe sleep, if she was lucky.

There was an empty house almost opposite Candy's, with an overgrown front garden.

'We could hide in here, innit?' said Links. 'So she don't see us. She'll only run away again, an' I'm done with chasin' her all over this island.'

He nudged the gate open and they all trooped in. They kept watch until dark but nobody came in or out of Candy's front door.

'We should take it in turns to sleep,' said Wills. 'I'll keep first watch and wake one of you when I feel tired.'

The others nodded gratefully and settled down. But before long, Wills felt his own eyes droop. Soon he was as soundly asleep as the others.

After their fruitless visit to Blackgang Chine, Chas and Arnie went back to Ventnor too. They parked their van in its usual spot near Ruth's house and waited and watched. It was quite late when she eventually arrived home but she still had the bag of money. Relieved that she hadn't managed to exchange it for the egg they relaxed and dozed off.

Indoors, Ruth was far from relaxed. She was trying vainly to contact Raven. To tell her that everything was fine, the sheep were out of the game. There was now nothing to stop a simple handover.

But Candy's phone was switched off.

Next morning, Ventnor was buzzing with excitement. The carnival procession would start at seven in the evening and everyone knew someone who was involved.

Candy woke feeling much better. She laced up her boots and went out to buy milk and bread for breakfast.

From their overgrown garden, the sheep watched her go. She wasn't carrying the pink bag.

'I'm so sorry I fell asleep,' Wills said for the umpteenth time.

'Forget it, tin-ribs,' said Links. 'You got us this far, innit.'

'Yes, dear,' said Sal kindly. 'And we are all poised to move like lightning when she does move the egg again.'

'Unless Oxo eats all the grass we're supposed to be hiding in,' said Jaycey, with a sniff.

Oxo took the hint and restrained himself, so the sheep remained hidden all day. Jaycey complained once about being bored, so to cheer her up Sal recited twenty of the less well-known verses from the Songs of the Fleece. Jaycey didn't complain again.

Ruth had spent a very restless night. She phoned Candy straight after breakfast but Candy's phone was still switched off. Ruth bit her lip and drummed her fingers on the kitchen table. She *had* to speak to Candy but she only had a phone number. She didn't know where she lived. Ruth drummed her fingers a bit longer then had a brain wave. She drove out to the dinosaur museum and asked Denzil Adams for Candy's address. Mr Adams was shocked. He couldn't *possibly* give a stranger the personal details of one of his staff. Next, Ruth tried the hairdresser's but Lisa was just as firm. She would never give a client's address. Not even to someone she respected as much as Miss Pemberton-Smith. Even though Candy's brother fancied her.

Angry and frustrated, Ruth drove home. She was aware of the Mr Fixall van following her. It had tailed her from the moment she left home. It had waited outside the museum and outside the hairdresser's. She parked by her house and watched the van park just along the road. The two men inside unfolded newspapers and pretended to be reading.

Ruth strode over, thumped the roof with her fist then banged hard on the window. Chas and Arnie jumped. Chas cautiously slid the window open.

'I know what you want,' shouted Ruth, 'but you're on your own now. Your sheep have been neutralised!'

186

'Eh?' said Arnie.

'You won't get the egg!'

'Egg . . .?' blustered Chas. 'What egg?'

Ruth glared at him. 'You tried to steal it at Alum Bay. And you were at Blackgang Chine yesterday. Why do you want it?'

'We could ask you the same,' said Arnie, leaning across Chas.

'How much do you want to just go away?' snapped Ruth suddenly.

Arnie's eyes lit up. 'How much you offering?'

'We're not going anywhere,' said Chas, nudging Arnie sharply aside. 'An' there's nothing you can do about it.'

'Right . . .' said Ruth. 'Right. But you'll regret it.' She stormed away, banging the side of van with her fist as she went.

'Brilliant!' said Arnie when she'd gone. 'You have just turned down the easiest money we're ever likely to make.'

'I've told you before,' said Chas, flicking open his paper. 'You have no aspirations.'

*

Arnie sulked all day. The brothers took turns to stretch their legs and go for food but by evening they were both bored and fed up. Arnie almost wished he was back in prison.

Then, just before seven, Ruth came out of the house. She was smartly dressed but still had the plastic carrier bag grasped firmly in one hand. She strode away on foot. Chas and Arnie followed in the van but at the end of the road their way was blocked by a line of plastic cones.

'You can't drive into town,' said a steward in a high-vis yellow tabard. 'The streets are closed to traffic until the carnival procession's finished.'

Chas leapt to the ground. 'Go and park somewhere,' he shouted at Arnie. 'Then come and find me.' He ran on, dodging his way through the crowds of people beginning to fill the streets. Ruth was almost out of sight.

Candy hadn't picked up her phone all day. She knew she had to talk to Enigmata eventually but she would do it when she was ready, not before. After hours of thinking and worrying she suddenly decided to go out. It was carnival night. She would go and watch the procession. She loved the carnival. It would take her mind off her worries. She found the plastic ice-cream tub full of small change she'd been putting aside all year for the charity buckets and tucked it into her pink bag. Then she rolled up her fleece and stuffed that in too. It would be chilly later. She laced on her boots and strode out of the door, feeling more like her old, jaunty self.

'Ohmygrass, ohmygrass . . . she's coming,' cried Jaycey, who was on watch. 'And she's got the egg!'

'Softly does it, innit,' whispered Links as they tip-hoofed from the overgrown garden. 'Bad news if she sees us.'

The Warriors followed Candy at a distance, treading as quietly as they could on the pavements. There were hardly any people out here on the outskirts of town. Everyone was already down in the centre. The procession had started, and Candy could hear the drums of the marching bands and the cheers of the crowds. She walked faster. She trotted. She forgot the troubles of the past few days, turned a corner, and ran down to join the fun.

'Run!' shouted Oxo. 'She's getting away!'

The Warriors all began to run but none of them got past the corner.

A policeman suddenly appeared, cycling towards them. He jumped off and slewed his mountain bike across the pavement in front of them.

'Well, well . . . You'll be the little lot that's been causing all the trouble,' he said. 'Best get you behind baaaas.' He laughed at his own joke. 'Baaaas . . . that's a good one.'

'Go round him, innit!' shouted Links.

He tried to do so but the policeman span his bike and wheeled it straight at the curly-fleeced animal. He was talking on his radio as he moved.

'Bit of back-up, please. Sharpish. I've got those barmy sheep up here in Ocean Road.'

Oxo charged straight at the bike. 'One for five and five for . . . ouch!'

The policeman had turned the front wheel and Oxo's head got stuck in the spokes. He pulled himself free, leaving a large chunk of fleece behind in the buckled wheel.

'Ohmygrass . . .' gasped Jaycey, trying to run

around the other side of the policeman. 'Bald is *never* a good look, Oxo.'

The policeman stuck out a leg and Jaycey shied away.

But it's hard to pen five sheep against a wall for long with only a buckled bike and eventually they galloped off, leaving the policeman sitting exhausted and sweating on the pavement, talking into his radio.

'In your own time,' he panted. 'I wouldn't want you to hurry or anything.'

The Warriors were free but the woman with the pink bag had disappeared. The noise of the bands and the laughter and cheering in the town centre were even louder now. But up here in the streets just above, there was not a soul in sight.

Suddenly Wills was overcome. 'We'll never find her now,' he cried. 'Or the egg. It could hatch at any minute and the world will be destroyed. And it will be all our fault!'

And for the first time in his life, Wills burst into tears.

16
Money ... Money ... Money

The carnival route was packed with people. They stood five deep on the pavements. They sat on the churchyard wall. They hung out of the windows of shops and houses on either side of the street. Some even climbed lamp posts for a better view.

Candy wriggled and squirmed her way through the crowd and found the best spot she could to watch the procession. She was five lines back, pressed against the churchyard wall, but she was quite tall and could see over most of the heads.

She clapped enthusiastically as one of the bands, dressed in smart uniforms, marched past, led by their drum major twirling his baton. The bandsmen and women clashed their cymbals, bashed their drums and blew their trumpets.

The Sandy Bay entry passed next. Its carnival

queen and her attendants, dressed as ice maidens, waved and smiled shyly from their ice blue castle. More floats came by and pirates shaking charity buckets walked alongside a galleon on wheels. Then Candy heard a roar of approval from the crowd further down the street. A Land Rover towing a huge float came slowly into view. The Land Rover was driven by old Fred Jolliff. Sitting next to him was an even older lady Candy didn't know. She was wrinkly and twinkly and was waving and smiling.

'That's the woman who designed the float,' someone in front of Candy said. 'Comes from the mainland. A place called Eppingham or something.'

The procession edged forward a little and now Candy and all those around her could see the float itself.

'WOW!'

Mouths dropped open. People stood on tiptoe to see better. They clapped and laughed.

The trailer had been dressed with twigs and straw to look like a nest. A dragon's nest. On each side of the nest lay half of a giant egg shell. And in the middle stood the newly emerged baby dragon.

Baby dragon? It was huge! It had overlapping green

and black scales, long claws and rows and rows of white teeth. Its red eyes swivelled from side to side. Its great wings flapped slowly up and down. And its nostrils puffed smoke!

'It's awesome!' breathed Candy. 'Just awesome!'

Everyone around agreed.

'Brilliant . . . Fabulous . . . Best ever . . . Never seen anything so good . . .'

The float came to a halt and now Candy and the others turned their attention to the people walking on either side of it. Not just any old people, though. They all had green faces with red-rimmed eyes, and green legs and arms. They wore green, glittery tunics, with thick tails pinned to their backs. And when they flapped their arms up and down, the wide green, gauzy fabric looked just like dragon wings. Music was beating from the float and the human dragons suddenly started to dance.

Candy could just hear a boy's voice shouting above all the other noise.

'Forward, back . . . forward, back . . . forward, back. Turn!'

The dancers all moved in time with each other

and the crowd cheered even louder.

'Can you shout it louder, Tod?' called one of the dancers.

'Three steps forward . . . Flap arms!' yelled Tod, from the back of the float.

Candy laughed, clapped and cheered along with everyone else. She took out a handful of coins and squeezed to the front of the crowd to toss them into the dragon's bucket.

And that was when she saw Ruth (code name Enigmata)!

Ruth was sitting in a large open-top car, next in line after the dragon float. A discreet notice on the car said that Rex Headland and Ruth Pemberton-Smith were the major sponsors of this year's Ventnor carnival. The car was driven by a uniformed chauffeur and Rex and Ruth were sitting side by side in the back. Rex was smiling and waving. But Ruth was staring straight at Candy.

Ruth suddenly stood up and beckoned urgently. Candy tried to back away but the crowd had closed behind her. Ruth opened the car door and beckoned again.

'Get in, if you're going, love,' said a woman on the

pavement next to Candy. 'You're standing right in front of the kids. They can't see through you.'

Candy dithered. She stepped into the road, intending to dodge around the car, but Ruth leaned out and grabbed her wrist. She had an iron grip for such a slight woman.

'Get in!' she ordered quietly. 'And smile.'

Candy half-climbed, was half-dragged into the car and found herself wedged between Rex and Ruth. Rex gave her a pleasant nod as they drove slowly on. Ruth resumed smiling and waving at the crowd.

'Why didn't you answer my calls?' demanded Ruth. She didn't wait for an answer. 'Never mind. I had a hunch you'd turn up tonight, so I brought the money.' She nodded at the dragon float in front of them. 'Rather fitting, isn't it?'

'I don't want the money,' said Candy.

'Don't be silly,' snapped Ruth. 'Of course you do. Now give me the egg.' She looked sharply down at the pink bag.

Candy shook her head. 'You don't understand . . .'

Rex suddenly turned to face Candy. He spoke quietly and earnestly.

'No, my dear. It's *you* who doesn't understand. You don't understand quite *why* I want the egg.'

'I don't *care* why *either* of you want it,' wailed Candy.

'Then you should.' Rex was staring ahead again. 'It's not about money. I'm not interested in that. It's about something far more important. The future of Great Britain.'

Candy stared at him.

'What I want,' continued Rex. 'Is to create a living dinosaur. Oh, I realise the chances are slim, but if anyone does it, it must be *me*.'

'Why?' whispered Candy. 'Why *you*?'

'Because I am the only person left who sees the truth. The government is useless. Our enemies are everywhere and getting stronger by the day. And nobody but me seems to see the danger. Maybe it takes an old military man to read the signs, to understand the secret signals. But it's a fact: no one has any idea how to defend our wonderful country any more.' Rex sat up very straight. 'But in the hour of need, *I* shall come to the rescue.'

'You will . . .?' Candy shrank back in her seat.

'I will. If I can create *one* living dinosaur, I can clone

more. A troop of them. An army!' Rex turned and peered into Candy's face. 'Imagine,' he said earnestly, 'how you'd feel if you were an enemy soldier, just landed on the beaches of Britain, and you saw a line of dinosaurs marching towards you.'

Candy gulped. 'Scared?'

'Exactly!' barked Rex. 'Scared. So scared you'd turn tail and run. I can train dogs, I can train horses, I can train men. Why not dinosaurs? A private army with which I will ensure the safety of our great and glorious land.'

Ruth held out the plastic bag full of cash. '*Now* give me the egg!' she snapped.

Before Candy could reply, somebody in the crowd screamed. The first scream was followed by others and then shouts and warnings and more screams.

Candy looked up and saw the thing she dreaded most. The ram with yellow eyes was standing on the church wall. It was staring straight at her. It was about to leap.

After Wills' moment of despair, it was Sal who had taken charge.

'We will find Pink Bag Woman, dear,' she said confidently. 'If in my long life I have learnt one thing about eggs, it is that they only ever roll downhill.'

'But it's in a bag,' pointed out Wills.

'Let's go, man,' said Links, distracted by the thump of the bands and sound systems. 'I can hear sweet music.'

A downhill minute later, the Warriors arrived in streets that were far from empty. They threaded their way through the throng of human legs and buggies towards the church then trotted across the churchyard. Now they were standing on the wall, looking over the heads of the crowd. They stared at the enormous, smoke-belching dragon, standing between the two halves of its cracked egg.

'Ohmygrassohmygrass . . . it's hatched! Hatched-hatchedhatched!'

'No!' cried Wills before Oxo could launch himself at the carnival float. 'That's not real! It's made of wire and stuff!'

'You's right, man,' said Links. 'That is a fake. Great music but a fake.'

'Yes,' said Wills. 'But look behind. In the car.'

They all looked and saw Candy in the car, clutching her pink bag on her lap.

'One for five and five for the pink bag . . .!' cried Oxo. The people on the pavement underneath him screamed and backed into each other to get out of his way as he launched himself from the wall. Oxo crashed on to the pavement with a thud, shook himself, then charged at the car. Ruth hadn't closed the door properly after she'd dragged Candy inside and now it was swinging open. Oxo headed straight for it, followed by his fellow Warriors.

Candy froze with fear. Then, as the ram reached the open door on one side of the car, she dived over Rex and hurled herself out of the other.

'Raven! Stop!' Ruth stood up and waved the carrier bag in the air. 'You're going without –'

The car rocked as Oxo scrabbled to get aboard.

'How did you get out!' Rex roared, slashing at the ram with his furled umbrella. 'Who opened the barn door?' As Oxo struggled and Rex slashed, the car rocked even faster. Ruth was lurching violently from side to side now, still holding the bag above her head.

'Don't drop that, old girl!' cried Rex, suddenly

turning his attention away from the animal trying to get into his car. He stuck out his furled umbrella to help steady the bag. But the point of the umbrella pierced the plastic and slit the bag right open. Thousands of bank notes fluttered into the air. They were caught on the warm evening breeze. They swirled and twirled and floated down like confetti at a wedding.

17
Scrambled Egg

Some people kept the money they caught, but most put it into the buckets the charity collectors were shaking.

'Never known a carnival like it,' said one of the collectors, as another handful of twenty pound notes was thrust into his bucket.

Candy was hardly aware of the money floating down from the sky. Her only thought was to get away from those sheep and especially *that* ram. She ducked through the crowd on the pavement and headed for one of the narrow side streets that led down to the beach.

Oxo didn't stop to look at the shocked and furious humans in the stationary car he'd just boarded.

'Ram coming through!' he shouted as he barged past Ruth and Rex, forcing them back into their seats.

He butted the opposite door open and leapt out.

'And a Jacob!' cried Jaycey. She leapt in easily and with one bound was out the other side.

Wills jumped a little too high and landed on Ruth's lap.

'Sorry about that . . .' he called as he leapt off and out after Oxo and Jaycey.

Sal struggled to clamber in but her legs were too short.

'I can't get in, I can't get in . . .' she bleated in a panic.

Links put his head under her bottom and shoved.

'Ooh!' Sal was catapulted on board and trampled over Ruth and Rex's feet without even noticing.

Links charged through after her. 'Way to go, Warriors!' he yelled as he and the other rare breeds galloped after Candy.

After they'd gone, Ruth and Rex sat in stunned silence for a moment, staring at their battered ankles.

'I did tell you what they were like,' said Ruth finally. 'Completely baaarmy.'

She and Rex abandoned their car and ran after the sheep.

Candy had gone only a few steps down the narrow side street when she was ambushed. She felt a sharp tug at her shoulder as a hand closed on the strap of her pink bag. She turned and found herself face-to-face with one of the men who'd been following her for days. The one with the cake-stained hoodie. He yanked the bag again and it slipped from Candy's shoulder. She left him holding it and carried on running.

Chas was amazed. Suddenly it was all becoming easy. He'd been dogging Ruth's footsteps since she left home. Hoping against hope that she would lead him to the girl with the dragon's egg. And she had!

He pulled out his phone and talked as he continued walking rapidly away from the main street.

'Arnie. Where are you?'

'Parked up the end of the seafront,' said Arnie. 'It was as close as I could get.'

'Start the engine,' ordered Chas. 'We're looking at a quick getaway.' He heard footsteps and glanced quickly over his shoulder. Five sheep and two humans were pounding along the pavement close behind him. Chas started running. 'Make that very quick. And open the back doors. I might need to dive in.'

Candy heard the chase behind her, turned and stopped running. She saw the man who'd stolen her bag flying downhill towards her with it clutched to his chest. The ram was close behind him and its yellow eyes weren't on Candy any more. They were firmly fixed on the thief. Candy suddenly realised that it wasn't *her* the animal was after. It was whoever was holding the pink bag! Relief washed over her. She veered off into a seaside shelter.

Oxo almost had his teeth in Chas's bottom when one of his hooves twisted in a pothole. He fell heavily and rolled over a couple of times.

'You all right, man?' shouted Links as he hurtled past.

'Nothing broken, I hope, dear . . .?' called Sal, also thundering by.

Jaycey and Wills, being the lightest, didn't have time to speak. Their hooves were hardly touching the ground. The sloping path was so steep now that all the sheep were out of control. Oxo picked himself up and rumbled after the rest.

'Man, we's goin' way too fast, innit . . .' cried Links.

'Ohmygrass . . .!' squealed Jaycey. She was only a nose away from the man with the bag. 'Ohmyhoovesohmyhorns,' she cried. 'What should I doooooooo?'

'Butt!' yelled Oxo. 'Butt him!'

Jaycey closed her eyes and butted. 'One for five and five for . . . ohmygrass!' Her horns bumped hard into the man's bottom.

Chas stumbled forward and the pink duffel bag flew from his hands as he fell.

'Noooo!' he wailed as it sailed up into the air. And then, 'Yessss!' as it shot straight through the open rear doors of the van. It landed with a heavy thump inside.

'Great throw, bruv!' yelled Arnie from beside the van.

Chas was scrambling to his feet. 'Drive! Drive!' he shouted at Arnie.

Close behind, Wills suddenly dug his hooves into the tarmac. Links, Sal and Oxo slammed into him at the bottom of the slope. Ruth and Rex swerved past, heading straight for the open van.

Jaycey saw that the others had stopped and scooted back to join them.

'What have we stopped for?' she cried. 'He's getting away again.'

'Brilliant butt, Jaycey,' panted Oxo.

'Yeah, top respect,' said Links.

'But it didn't *work*,' wailed Jaycey. 'He's still got the egg!'

'Um, worse than that, guys,' breathed Wills. He was staring at the van. 'I think it's going to hatch!'

They all looked. Then listened for a moment. A rumbling, bubbling, creaking noise was coming from inside the van. The sheep turned and ran a little way back up the hill.

Arnie had heard the noise too. He was still standing by the driver's door with the engine running.

'What are you waiting for?' yelled Chas, from the passenger side of the van. He seemed not to have noticed the noise.

The rumbling grew louder.

'It *sounds* like a volcano . . .' said Ruth who had finally come to a stop beside Arnie. She turned to Rex, puzzled.

Rex nodded. 'And it's about to erupt, my dear . . . Get away!' he suddenly barked. 'Back up the hill!'

But it was too late. The van had begun to rock from side to side. Smoke belched from the rear doors.

The rumbling, creaking, bubbling inside became a roar. Then:

BOOM!

The roof of Mr Fixall's chemical-filled van burst open. Jets of gloopy white and yellow liquid shot high in the air. Then rained down all over Chas and Arnie, Ruth and Rex.

'Ohmygrass . . .' cried Jaycey, backing further up the slope. 'It stinks!'

'Yeh. Just like rotten eggs, innit,' said Links.

Wills stared in wonder. Then turned excitedly. 'Do you think that was it, Sal?' he asked. 'Have we done it? Have we smashed the dragon's egg?'

Sal had no doubt at all. The Songs of the Fleece were never wrong. The evidence was there before their eyes. She stood tall and began to recite:

'If sheeply Warriors brave and true,
Can find the egg and *break* it too,
They first will see an awful sight:
Dragon's yolk and dragon's white.

208

The shattered dragon's egg will *stink*,

Will make them choke and make them blink.

But they should stand with heads held high:

The plague of dragons *will not fly*!'

She smiled round at them all. 'Does that answer the question?'

'High hooves!' cried Wills. And they all clacked hooves together.

Beyond the smoky, smelly silence, the sounds of the carnival up in the town continued.

'But you gotta admit,' said Links, 'not all dragons is bad. Them pretend ones on the street had some cool moves, innit.'

He looked hopefully at Sal and the others. A moment later, the Warrior Sheep were scampering back up the hill.

Chas and Arnie, Ruth and Rex stood where they were, beside the smoking, shattered van. They coughed and spluttered and vainly tried to brush paint, oil and all sorts of nasty chemicals from their faces, hair and clothes.

Ruth spotted a policeman with a wobbly front

wheel cycling towards them.

'Time to go, Uncle,' she whispered.

And with that, they slipped quietly away.

Chas and Arnie didn't notice them go. They were still staring at the wrecked van.

'Does this vehicle belong to you, sirs?'

Chas and Arnie jumped. They hadn't noticed the policeman either.

'Yes,' said Chas.

'No,' said Arnie.

The policeman gave them a look. He wasn't in the best of moods. 'I'll take that as an attempt to obstruct the course of justice.'

'Look,' said Chas, 'if it's about those nosey Golden Oldies – the ones who reported us for carrying sheep in the back of the van. Well, we didn't know they were there. The sheep, that is.'

The policeman nodded. 'Since you mention it, we *do* have a report from a member of the public concerning alleged cruelty to livestock.' He paused. 'But that is not our prime concern at the moment.'

'Oh,' said Arnie. 'That's all right, then.'

'No,' said the policeman, enjoying himself now.

'A van with this registration number has been reported missing from an address in London. Would you know anything about that?'

Chas glared at Arnie. 'You said he was on holiday for two weeks. Spain, you said.'

Arnie shrugged. 'Perhaps it rained and he came home early.'

The policeman interrupted by speaking into his radio.

'I need a van to bring in a couple of suspects,' he said. 'And a pick-up truck. And a hazardous waste disposal team. In your own time, of course.'

Rex and Ruth were halfway up the slope when they saw Candy. She leapt out of the seaside shelter and planted herself firmly in front of them.

'What happened?' she demanded. 'Where's my bag?'

'Blown to smithereens,' snapped Rex. 'Along with the dinosaur egg. And it's all your fault.'

'Rubbish!' Candy glared at them both.

Ruth looked back, coldly. 'What d'you mean, rubbish?'

'I tried to tell you in the car,' said Candy. 'But would you listen?' She drew a deep breath. 'The egg wasn't in my bag.'

Ruth and Rex stared at her. For several seconds.

'Where is it, then?' asked Ruth.

'Yes, my dear,' said Rex smoothly, suddenly hopeful. 'Do we still have our little arrangement? I can easily get more money.'

'I don't want your money,' said Candy. And the egg – the Neovenator's egg – is back in the museum.'

There was another stunned silence. Candy looked defiantly at Ruth and Rex.

'I slipped back last night and popped it in the wheelie bin. Then this morning I phoned Mr Adams.' She suddenly started to sob. 'He was really, really kind. He said we all make mistakes, and he wasn't going to prosecute me and I could even keep my job if I want it. And I sooooo do want it. It was the best job in the world. Interesting and useful and important. Finding out about the past . . .' She sobbed again.

Rex and Ruth stared at Candy in total disbelief.

'I'm so sorry, Uncle,' Ruth said at last. 'I did my best but it wasn't good enough.'

'Not your fault, old girl,' said Rex. 'People just don't understand how desperately important our mission is.' He nodded brusquely at Candy then turned away. 'Even when it's spelled out to them!'

Rex and Ruth marched back up the hill, their heads held high.

'I've been thinking about those sheep . . .' said Rex as they walked.

Ruth shuddered. She would very much rather not think about them.

'Odd creatures . . .' said Rex. 'Worked together all the time. Like a tip-top army unit. And if one flock can do it . . .'

Ruth was hurrying to keep up now. 'You think you could use *sheep* instead of dinosaurs to defend us from attack?'

'Why not? I'd need lots of them, of course. And they'd have to be well trained . . .' His pace quickened. 'Come on, old girl. I've got around three hundred sheep out in the top field. We start tomorrow!'

Up in the town, the carnival procession had almost reached the end of its route when the Warriors caught up with it. They wriggled and squeezed their way to the front of the crowd and stood on the edge of the pavement to watch. The dragon's float was coming. The humans around them cheered and shouted.

'Look!' cried Wills above all the noise. 'In that Land Rover pulling the dragon. It's Ida!'

He bounded across the road and sprang on to the bonnet.

Fred Jolliff braked and Wills sprang over the windscreen into Ida's lap.

'Well knock me down wi' a chicken feather,' exclaimed Fred. 'Where did 'ee come from?'

Jaycey, Sal, Links and Oxo hurried into the road after Wills.

'They've done it again, Gran!' cried Tod, who'd jumped down from the float to be with the sheep. 'What have they been up to this time?'

Ida didn't have a chance to reply. One of the carnival stewards was shouting.

'Keep moving, Fred. You're holding up the procession.'

Wills jumped out of the Land Rover and Tod shooed the sheep back towards the trailer.

'Get on to the float,' he said. 'You can ride beside the dragon.'

The Warriors stood proudly together on the trailer for the rest of the evening. The dragon's giant wings flapped slowly above their heads, smoke puffed from its nostrils and the music pumped from the speakers.

'This is so cool . . .' yelled Wills.

'Yeah, but we can make it cooler still, man,' said Links and he began to sing.

'We listened up good to the warning song,
'Bout how it would all go horribly wrong,
If the dragon's egg was allowed to hatch,
'Cos even our posse would be no match
For the deadly beasts that lurked inside:
A zillion dragons with scaly hides.
With teeth and claws and breathin' fire,
The future of the world was dark and dire.
But the Warrior Sheep can proudly tell,
That we found that egg and we scrambled it well!
Yeah, we found that egg and we scrambled it well!
High Hooves!'